STEPPING THROUGH MY NIGHTMARES

Stepping Through My Nightmares

A true story of fear and hope set against the backdrop of the Gulf War

Sheila Barlow
with David Waite

Hodder & Stoughton
LONDON SYDNEY AUCKLAND

Copyright © Sheila Barlow with David Waite 1998

First published in Great Britain 1998

The right of Sheila Barlow with David Waite to be identified
as the Authors of the Work has been asserted by them in
accordance with the Copyright, Designs and Patents Act 1988.

10 9 8 7 6 5 4 3 2 1

British Library Cataloguing in Publication Data
A CIP Catalogue record for this title
is available from the British Library

ISBN 0 340 69456 4

Typeset by Hewer Text Ltd, Edinburgh
Printed and bound in Great Britain by
Mackays of Chatham PLC, Chatham, Kent

Hodder and Stoughton
A Division of Hodder Headline PLC
338 Euston Road
London NW1 3BH

To Peter, Andrew and Laura with deepest love and gratitude for allowing me to share my story, therefore inevitably also telling part of theirs. For all the dear friends I have met along the way who have enriched my life and continue to brighten even my dullest of days, I give thanks . . .

> but those who hope in the Lord
> will renew their strength
> they will soar on wings like eagles;
> they will run and not grow weary
> they will walk and not faint.
> (Isaiah 40:31)

And to the one who is the wind beneath my wings I give my special thanks and dedicate this book.

Contents

1

A Family Divided

The hand on the bedside clock had just moved to five o'clock when the doorbell started to ring. I opened my eyes in disbelief. Five o'clock in the morning – who could be at the door at this hour? I glanced at my husband Peter, who was obviously still deeply asleep, and without a second thought got out of bed. The morning sun had not yet started its daily task of warming up the air, and I shivered slightly as I felt the effects of the air conditioning, which had been noisily working away throughout the night. Putting on my housecoat, I moved as quickly and quietly as I could to the front door, hoping that the children would not wake.

The thought crossed my mind as I walked towards the door that our early morning caller might not even be wanting to speak to our family. The army house which we were using had originally been allocated to friends of ours who had gone to America for a short holiday. We were 'house sitting' for them until our return to the UK in three weeks' time.

I opened the door cautiously, but I needn't have been alarmed. Standing in the yard, looking concerned and apologetic, was our friend Michael, who was in charge of running the British army camp where we were now living. He was a big man, a typical rugby player. I noticed that his normally neat mousy hair was slightly ruffled. Dressed in tee-shirt and shorts, he looked concerned and businesslike all at once. He began speaking quickly, with an urgency in his voice.

'Hello, Sheila. Sorry to call at this unearthly hour, but I've heard some disturbing news that Peter ought to know about. A few hours ago Iraqi troops came over the border, and Kuwait and Iraq are now on a war footing. I'll try and arrange a meeting for 6.00 a.m. so everyone will know what's going on and what they are expected to do.'

Before I had chance to ask him any other questions, he made his apologies and dashed off, anxious to alert as many people as possible. I muttered a word of thanks and began to close the door, but as I did so my eyes involuntarily strayed to the Kuwaiti oil refinery which stood next to the camp, separated only by a wire fence. I preferred not to think of the dangers everyone on camp faced by living in the chalet-type houses which made up the army base, most of which were of 90 per cent wooden construction. There wasn't much else on the base, really. A tiny shop, the Sergeants' Mess, a swimming pool, a tennis court, a video library and an access to the sea from the fenced-off beach. The fence was to stop local people wandering into the camp, which would not have been allowed from a security point of view, and which also meant that we were out of sight of the locals and therefore could wear Western clothes in this Islamic society.

The British military compound that had been our home for the past two years was small enough for everyone to know each other, and we all enjoyed helping one another out when we could. That was one of the reasons why we were living in the house of our friends, Vicki and Martin. They had decided to take a holiday in America to escape the extreme heat of the Kuwaiti summer, which meant that

2

we could use their home while we cleaned and packed up our house, without having to live in it at the same time, prior to returning to the UK. I shivered again as I thought of the ground-to-air missiles that guarded the oil refinery, and knew that I needed to put from my mind all feelings of panic and remain calm. For Peter, for our children Andrew and Laura, for us all.

Peter had been posted to Kuwait some two years earlier, and I, along with our two children, had accompanied him. It's never easy living away from family and friends, but we had enjoyed it well enough, and were now feeling excited about returning to the UK. And now this, so soon before our return home.

Peter was awake by the time I returned to the bedroom, the sound of the doorbell and the urgency in Michael's voice taking all thoughts of sleep from his mind. I quickly told Peter what had happened, and I could see his military training beginning to take over. I admired the way he always reacted in such a calm and controlled way in difficult situations. I wished I could do the same. Anyone looking at me might have *thought* so, but inside my stomach was churning and my mind was trying to make some sense of the situation in which I now found myself.

As we tried to assess the best thing to do next, we could clearly hear in the background the distant sounds of huge explosions that began to shake our flimsy house. In spite of this our children, ten-year-old Andrew and Laura, who was seven, slept until 8.00 a.m. quite oblivious to these new developments unravelling around them; being used to army manoeuvres going on from time to time, they didn't seem unduly concerned about the noises that greeted them when they woke up. Both Peter and I thought the world of our children. Andrew was of slight build, with blond hair, blue eyes and a mischievous grin on his face most of the time.

Self-assured and adventurous, in many ways he took after his dad. Laura also had fair hair, but it was a shade darker than Andrew's. She had a quiet, friendly personality and a happy, gentle nature.

Peter was summoned to a meeting, which gave me some time on my own to get my thoughts together and to try and deal with the churning I still felt inside. Thankfully, the local telephones were still functioning, so it was possible to contact other friends who were also in the army or air force and living in flats elsewhere, and we were able to stay in touch with the British Embassy, which gave us some comfort.

Soon Peter returned, and carefully went over the information that he had been given. As we sat drinking tea from Vicki's mugs, seated on the fawn-coloured settee in the lounge, he told me that the Iraqi army had come across the border with Kuwait at two in the morning. They came in huge numbers, taking Kuwait by storm, meeting with little resistance from the Kuwaiti army, who were no match for them and were quickly overcome.

As this battle went on at the border, helicopters and tanks were fighting a battle in the city. Later we were to discover that many of our friends were witnesses to this initial onslaught, and as the conflict continued they were able to keep us updated by telephone.

Soon the local grapevine went into action, and we heard that the British Embassy had announced that the Kuwaiti royal family had fled the country before hostilities had begun, and were now safe in Saudi Arabia. But that didn't stop the royal palace from coming under siege, defended only by a small group of Kuwaiti guards, assisted by one of the prince's brothers. We were shocked to discover that he had been killed, and the palace burnt and destroyed. It seemed that Iraqi troops were advancing fast across

Kuwait, taking some prisoners but killing many more in their search for ex-police officers, Kuwaiti military and anyone of importance, by this time probably deep in hiding.

As I started to prepare breakfast for the children, trying to behave as normally as I could, Peter told me the advice that everyone was being given by the British Embassy.

'They say the best thing is to sit tight and await further instructions,' he said, in a matter-of-fact voice which didn't really sound convincing. I smiled back at him, trying to feel as optimistic as he sounded. It gave me no comfort that our base was less than forty-five minutes from the Saudi border, which was in the opposite direction from the hostilities going on.

It was a strange day. We carried on, trying to act as normally as possible, if only for the children's sake. They were very good, but not very impressed when told that they couldn't go and play outside. They were only normally 'grounded' if they had done something wrong. Peter had been trained to take military orders and obey them. But the children hadn't, and neither had I.

Every so often we would hear the sound of guns and wonder what the next few hours would bring. Even though Peter would never admit it, I guessed he was weighing up the possibilities of escape, in spite of orders to the contrary. The official line was that the British Embassy was working out a plan to evacuate the British citizens, and I knew that Peter and the other British military personnel would be instrumental in putting this plan into action as soon as the opportunity arose.

Nothing was now certain. We had no idea whether we would have to sit tight in this house, or suddenly be asked to move at a moment's notice. Knowing that I would feel better if we had some provisions to hand, we gathered some food and containers of bottled water together, ready to grab if the orders came through for us to move. The occasional enemy aircraft flying overhead was a grim reminder that anything could happen at any time.

The telephone rang intermittently. We shared a line with our next-door neighbours, Jackie and Gerry. The phone seemed to have a new urgency each time it sprang into life. Sometimes it was Jackie, wondering how we were, then the British Embassy would call, with new information or instructions. We had just decided to have another cup of tea when an Embassy official got in touch and suggested that we should start packing our belongings into boxes. I suspected that this was to keep us busy rather than for any practical purpose, but at least it stopped us just sitting around and brooding. Peter and I had already packed our things, and with any luck they were now on a ship bound for England. It seemed logical, therefore, to try and save as many of the personal things belonging to Vicki and Martin as we could, since we were in their home.

Trying to put myself in their shoes, I began to collect what I thought they would have wanted to pack, given the chance. It felt awkward, packing up someone else's house for them, but we did it as thoughtfully as we could, even taking some photos out of their frames so that I could carry them with me, in order that they would at least have some memories of their children to keep. Peter meanwhile started to sort out some of their important papers – birth certificates, bank details and the like. He also felt uncomfortable going through their private things, but what else could he do?

As it turned out, our careful packing, both of our own belongings and of those of our friends, was to no avail. News came to us a few days later that because of red tape our belongings had not been shipped to England after all, but had remained at the dockside, awaiting clearance. On the first day of the conflict the entire contents had been blown sky-high, resulting in the loss of nearly everything that we owned. And although we didn't know it then, we were ultimately to learn that Vicki and Martin didn't get any of the boxes I had packed, either.

Although I tried to keep calm, my nerves were constantly on edge as I expected something to happen at any moment. Eventually it was time to go to bed. I felt mentally exhausted, but sleep didn't come easily; finally we drifted off. I couldn't have known then that this would be the last time I would sleep in a bed for more than two hours at a time for the next two weeks.

The next day dawned all too soon, and apart from the uncertainty of the situation around us we had another problem to face – Andrew and Laura's boredom! They hated staying indoors for no real reason that they could see, and I knew that we would have to think of something. They had watched the videos that we had borrowed from the base's video shop several times, and there was no chance of getting any new ones for the moment! Besides, it was doing none of us any good being cooped up in this house, and I could see that Peter was getting restless, too.

The monotony was broken for a while when Rosie came to pick up some of her belongings. Rosie was Vicki and Martin's Filipino maid, who sometimes slept over when Vicki had extra work for her to do. Instead of staying around and chatting, she picked up some clothes she had left behind, made her excuses and left. We discovered later that she was about the last person to leave the camp before the gates were shut, and no one was allowed in or out from then on.

Suddenly Peter announced, 'I'm going to take the children swimming!' I looked at him open-mouthed, sure that he couldn't really be serious but knowing that he was, as he wouldn't have said such a thing within earshot of the children otherwise. In minutes they were ready to leave the house, and Peter left me with some unforgettable words ringing in my ears: 'Don't worry, it'll be all over in twenty-four hours. Trust me!'

Now that the house was empty, with the chatter of the children absent for a while, I could hear the sound of sporadic gunfire and explosions getting nearer all the time. Suddenly my thoughts were interrupted by the telephone ringing again. It was the British Embassy, keeping us in touch again with the latest situation. But by now we knew that all communications were being monitored by the Iraqis and we had to be careful what we said.

I turned on the radio, which was permanently tuned to the BBC World Service, to see what other bits of news I could glean. A report stated that a jumbo jet on its way from London to Delhi and Kuala Lumpur, carrying 367 passengers, had been encouraged to land in Kuwait for refuelling and was now being held on the runway. Things were beginning to escalate and the Allied troops were now being flown across to the Saudi–Kuwait border, ready to repel and attack the Iraqi invaders. The Americans were talking about air attacks. Things were not looking good. I tried to keep myself occupied with things to do and decided to get on with some more packing.

After what seemed like an age, Peter and the children returned from their swimming trip, having had a good time – and with more news. The Kuwaiti guards on our camp entrance were frightened for their lives, so some of our men had given them civilian clothing to enable them to leave. We didn't blame them for wanting to get away, and anyway the last thing we wanted was a conflict. After they had gone, one of our men put up a Union Flag at the entrance so that the Iraqi soldiers would know that we were British and not a Kuwait army unit.

Probably because of the swimming which had worn them out, the children made no fuss about going to bed earlier than usual that night. Peter, dressed in just shorts and a tee-shirt, with flip-flops dangling on his feet, decided to use the evening to look through some more documents. It was eight o'clock, and even though the sun had disappeared from the sky a few hours before, the house was still warm. I began to relax for the first time since I had answered the door to Michael. I had just put the kettle on for another drink when suddenly the camp siren rang out, a pre-arranged signal to call the men to a meeting.

Peter left quickly, not bothering to change, concerned not to miss out on any new information that might have become available. I watched him disappear into the night, and then went back into the lounge, trying to decide what to be getting on with until he returned. Suddenly there was a loud thump on the door. Thinking that it might be one of Peter's colleagues, I rushed to open it, to be met by two very irate Iraqi soldiers brandishing kalashnikov rifles. They couldn't speak any English, but nevertheless started to shout at me, and I knew they were looking for Peter. I saw the anger in their eyes, and smelt their stale breath as they shouted in my face. I was terrified. I was on my own, completely defenceless, with two small children fast asleep in their bedrooms; these men could do whatever they wanted to me or my kids. I yelled back at them, wishing that I knew some of their language, shouting that Peter had left. To my relief they left without forcing their way into my house. I learnt later that other households weren't so fortunate, as some soldiers had gone straight through the front door, boot first, and, finding the men, knocked them around with their rifles before shoving them forcibly out of the houses with the families looking on.

I was shaking as I closed the door, wondering what on earth I should do next. I grabbed the phone and called a friend, who told me that all the men on camp had been bussed away, out of the gates and into the blackness of the night.

I slumped into a sofa, feeling all the strength drain out of me. I knew that this was no disciplined army, more a bunch of louts enjoying a sudden feeling of power. Peter had left the house so suddenly, without any proper goodbye – now I wondered if I would ever see him again. How would the children react? I knew that there was no one on the camp who could protect us. Outside I could hear the sounds of soldiers scuffling past and the occasional gunfire in the town nearby. I felt completely weak and helpless.

Peter had been trained for war situations, but not me – I was just your everyday housewife and mother! Fear coursed through my body, and every sense that I possessed screamed within me. Fear seemed to be all around me, like a consuming giant that I had no control over. What other terrors lay ahead for us all? I knew that I had to repress my feelings and be strong, but that was going to be easier said than done. I had never felt so alone or afraid as I did now. What on earth did the next day hold for us all?

2

Reflections

My childhood never gave any clues as to how my life would work out as an adult. Born on 9 March 1952, I was the second child of Edith and Charles Sayers. Their first child was also a girl, Anne, and six years after my birth my brother Richard was born, completing our family.

We lived in the country in a three-bedroomed detached house surrounded by a garden. My father was employed as a gardener, and the house came with the job. Mum also had green fingers, and she kept our small plot of land in wonderful shape. The outside of the house was painted pink, giving it a warm, cosy atmosphere. Downstairs consisted of a reasonably large front room, which was only used at special times of the year such as Christmas, when more space was needed; a rip-roaring fire, going halfway up the chimney, would make the otherwise cold room warm and inviting. Mostly, though, we used the kitchen/diner where we would spend the majority of our time. It had a nice coal fire, which made it a favourite place for the whole family to congregate.

In those carefree times, which will probably never return, children were free to roam the countryside during holidays and at weekends, enjoying every moment of the outdoor life. Although we never had a lot of money or expensive toys, we found great enjoyment in simple pleasures, like making dens in the woods out of leaves and fallen branches, picking wild flowers, and, in the autumn, going on a hunt for blackberries that Mum would make into delicious blackberry and apple pies and jam.

She always reckoned that I was worse than any boy. The problem was that I loved to climb trees. They seemed to present a challenge to me, which I just couldn't resist. But I could never understand how trees always proved to be easier to get up than down! This caused extra work for both my parents. My father frequently had to rescue me from high branches that I had got stuck in, and then, after I had gone to bed, my mother would have to get out the needle and thread to mend my torn clothes.

Sunday mornings would not find me up a tree, but in the local Anglican church. I loved the hymns that were sung in the services, but little else. Although the little church building was pretty, it held no real attraction for me. For one thing, I was the only child who ever seemed to attend the services. The elderly congregation numbered about twenty souls, nearly all of them over fifty, and most nearer seventy! There was no Sunday School, and the sermons went way over my head. The church was cold most of the time, being much too expensive to heat. After the service the grown-ups exchanged a few brief words before rushing off home to see what stage their roast joints of meat had arrived at! As churchgoers, they rarely saw each other in the week, so brief words were their only form of fellowship. I learnt to believe that God existed but that was about all. I had no concept of His love for me. In spite of all this, I never stopped going to church completely, but my attendance gradually got less and less.

School was much more fun, in spite of the fact that I struggled with some of the classes. I loved physical exercise, so I concentrated on all aspects of sport rather than dry and dusty school work. And my dedication paid off. Before I knew it I was representing the school at hockey, rounders, athletics, netball and cross-country running. I was getting fitter and fitter, and having a whale of a time. Even the teachers didn't seem too concerned about the lack of academic progress I was making – but my mother was.

As I was tucking into some of her home-made cake one evening she said, 'Sheila, the reports that your dad and I are getting from school about your progress aren't too good. We're pleased, of course, that you're doing so well at sport, but what's going to happen when it's time to find a job . . . ?' I shrugged my shoulders, and her voice trailed off, as she didn't have any more answers than I did. Something would turn up, I reckoned, and in any case there was no point in worrying. The school system then was such that unless a child had shown real academic ability and wanted to stay on at school for a further year to sit examinations, they would be expected to leave school at fifteen. Needless to say, I left at fifteen!

My first job was in the baby department of Boots the Chemist in Taunton. Although the work was quite hard, I enjoyed contact with the mums and their infants. It was fun helping to weigh the babies, and meeting so many different people. But after a while the job settled down into a fairly predictable routine, and I began to think that a change might not be a bad idea.

The answer to this problem came from an unexpected source. Mrs Stewart-Wilson, a friend of the family, who had known me since childhood, asked if I would consider becoming a nanny for her two children, six-year-old Alice and three-year-old Sophy. I felt that I would enjoy working for her, noting her bubbly personality and happy smile. But there was one snag. Well, two actually. The first was that

Mrs Stewart-Wilson's husband was a colonel in the British army and was now serving in Germany, so I would have to leave home and the area I had known all my life in order to take up this post. As a seventeen-year-old, this didn't pose many problems. I was happy at home, but saw this as my chance of seeing a bit of the world. Germany wasn't that far away, I reasoned, and I could soon get home if the going got too tough.

The other bridge that I had to cross before being able to take up the job offer was more unusual. Mrs Stewart-Wilson had asked if I objected to being confirmed in the Church of England as a prerequisite for this appointment. Excited at the idea of a new life in a foreign country, I accepted almost immediately, without really thinking too deeply about the consequences.

Even though my knowledge of God at this stage was practically zero, I saw no reason why I shouldn't be confirmed. In fact, I took this commitment seriously. I rather looked forward to the classes, hoping that I might learn more about God, and clear some of the confusion I had about many things concerning Him. He had remained distant to me in the preceding years in spite of my wanting to know more about Him and the effect He might have on my daily life.

Following my confirmation I was able to receive communion, but it had brought me no further forward in the spiritual quest. However, all thoughts that I might have had of knowing more about spiritual things quickly took a back seat as I packed my bags for Germany and my new life.

My new home was a large grey detached house with a good-sized square garden at the rear. It was in an area where other army families lived, so it was like being in a little English enclave in the heart of Germany. It had four large bedrooms, plus another large bedroom, which had been turned into a nursery. This room became quite important to me, as I spent a lot of my time there, both in the daytime and then again when the children had gone to bed.

Feeling apprehensive and excited all at the same time, I soon settled in to life as Alice and Sophy's nanny. Six months later, Belinda arrived on the scene, adding to my responsibilities. The children were lovely, and lots of hard work, but that meant that I didn't have time to think too much about the homesickness that I felt at first. The winter was cold, with lots of thick snow, and the children and I had great fun rolling snow into huge balls that we then made into snowmen. The girls would squeal with delight as I added the final touches of a carrot nose and coal eyes.

I found that I quickly made friends with girls who were nannies like me. We would try and work it so our days off coincided, and then go to a nearby English-speaking cinema, buying a delicious roll of bread with an enormous frankfurter in the middle afterwards. Life became fun, with new friends, lots of parties and new places to explore.

The days took on what became a familiar routine. In the morning I would get Alice ready for school, then walk her to the bus stop and put her on the school bus. Half an hour later, I would be back at the bus stop, this time with Sophy, who went to kindergarten each morning. I would then go back to the house to make the beds, tidy the rooms, do some washing and ironing – and prepare lunch. How I wished I had taken more notice when Mum was getting our meals ready back home. Timing different foods so they were all ready together was an art in itself, but in spite of my inexperience in culinary matters I was soon turning out things like shepherd's pie and macaroni cheese which the children seemed to enjoy, much to my relief.

My morning chores completed, it would be time to pick

up Sophy from the bus stop again. In the afternoon I would often take her to a nearby duck pond, where we would enjoy watching the ever-hungry ducks feed on the bread that we took for them before rushing home to prepare tea. There was usually just enough time to have a little play with the children before bathtime came round for them, and another busy day came to a close. In the evenings I played records in the nursery or read a book, never bothering with the television, which only transmitted German programmes which I didn't understand.

Sunday was a working day for me, so in spite of the fact that Mrs Stewart-Wilson had requested that I be confirmed before taking up the job as nanny, apart from the occasional Sunday I only attended church at Christmas and Easter! I had several attempts at reading the Bible, but it seemed to be written in another language, and I had little success in understanding it. Wading through the first few chapters of the Old Testament, I learnt that in the beginning God created the world. From the things I heard in church I learnt that Jesus had died on a cross, but nothing seemed relevant to me.

But I soon had other things to occupy my mind. The Stewart-Wilsons were on the move again – back to England, in fact – and I of course returned with them. My stint abroad had lasted only six months, but it had been a time when I had grown up in many ways, including getting my first boyfriend.

James was with the Scots Guards, batman to one of the officers down the road from where I lived. He was everything a girl could wish for. Tall, dark – and handsome! We went out together for a few months, and when I returned to England the relationship continued. He came back from Germany about the same time as I did, but he lived quite a way away and seeing each other on a regular basis proved difficult. Then to my surprise, one day he asked me to marry him. Taken aback, I said that I just felt I was too young to settle down. He left soon after, and that was the last time I saw my handsome batman. But I was still very young, and there was my new life in Britain to get used to.

We returned to a house in London, in a row of other houses, and I really enjoyed living in the capital city, with so much to see and do. I stayed with the family for five years, by which time the children needed far less care, so the day came when I sadly packed my bags and moved on. However, I still kept in touch with them and saw them from time to time, including attending all three girls' weddings over the last few years.

My new family were living in the Cotswolds in a lovely country house, with a nice garden and, importantly for me, a good nursery. I really felt that was important, as I didn't want to spend my free time with the family I was working for, however well I got on with them. The family consisted of Mr and Mrs Wills and their son Michael. This suited me fine, as I wanted fewer than three children to look after. I knew, of course, that Mrs Wills was expecting a child in a few months' time, but that was not a problem to me. It was a shock, therefore, when Mrs Wills gave birth to twins, Clare and Edward, and I was back to looking after three children again!

Rather than being less busy I was worked off my feet as Edward was a Down's Syndrome child, and needed extra care and attention. In spite of all the hard work that his disability caused me, I gained so much from that little boy, his plucky courage showing me that it's possible to be happy and loving no matter what problems we might be going through. I also have great respect for all the family and how they managed to come to terms with their setbacks and stick together in the difficult times. Little did I know how much I would need to know these things as the events of my life unfolded.

I soon found a new friend in the form of Christine. She too was a nanny, working for a family who lived quite some distance away. Our families knew each other, so we would enjoy each other's company when a joint lunch or tea party was arranged between them. On other occasions we would try and get the same day off, and spend time together in my new-found pride and joy – a dark green Hillman Imp! In spite of the fact that it was very temperamental and only started when it wanted to, I loved that little car, and Christine and I would go exploring in it, in spite of Christine's total lack of sense of direction, which we shared many a good laugh about. Sometimes we would go to a cinema, or find some pretty village to wander round, before going back to Christine's place where she introduced me to the delights of toasted banana sandwiches!

Christine and I were alike in so many ways, not just in our job – even our height was identical. There was one big difference though. Christine was engaged to be married. Her husband-to-be, Robin, was an army corporal serving in Germany. I was thrilled when she asked me to be one of her bridesmaids, and before we knew it the Big Day had arrived. Robin and Christine made a wonderful couple, but I had more than a passing interest in Peter, Robin's best man. Peter was average to short in height, slight of build, with brown, slightly wavy hair. He seemed to have a happy-go-lucky air about him. A well-organised sort of chap, with lots of self-confidence, he had a positive attitude to life. I got the impression that he wouldn't suffer fools gladly, in spite of his extrovert personality.

Peter too was in the army in Germany, but in spite of this romance blossomed between us. Before we knew it, wedding bells were in the air for us. Everyone was thrilled with our news, but then two weeks before the ceremony Peter asked for the wedding to be postponed. He loved me, and I loved him, but he had some unanswered questions in his mind about what he was doing. Peter had become a Christian about two years before we met, and was increasingly concerned that his proposed new bride might not be able to share this very important part of his life. At this point he was also in the process of being posted back to England as a sergeant, and the pressures of a new job, together with the other niggling doubts, brought him to the point where he felt it best to postpone the wedding. Although tearful, I understood, and felt that everything would work out if I gave him the space he needed.

My parents, however, didn't react in the same way. In fact, along with almost everyone else they were very, very angry with Peter. The only person who didn't seem to be angry with him was me, in spite of the fact that I had already given up my job, in order to prepare for marriage. Poor Peter, he just wanted to get things right, but at one point it seemed as though everyone had turned against him.

In the end, though, everything turned out all right. Peter put his doubts behind him, and we got married nine months after the original date. Life was to change again, although I had no idea just how deep those changes were going to be. Maybe it was just as well that I didn't.

3

New Challenges to Face

Once married, I began to adjust to life as an army wife. Our first house together, on an army base in England, left much to be desired: it was very small, very cold and very bleak. Like all the other houses around us, it was furnished with army-issue furniture, which was adequate but pretty awful. I wondered at first if I would ever get used to the camouflage-green covers on the cushions and chairs! But they do say that love overcomes all things, and I made the best of what we had been given, and enjoyed our life together. I was with the man I loved, and he was doing the kind of work that he had chosen to do. What more could we ask for?

Eighteen months after we moved into our first home, our first child, Andrew, was born. Life was now very busy again, as children are always hard work, but this time it was *my* child I was looking after. Our happiness was short-lived, however, as Peter was posted to Belize for five months just six weeks after the birth. Separation is part of life when one is married to a soldier, and I gradually got used to the idea, but that does not mean that I ever liked it!

I suddenly became, to all intents and purposes, a one-parent family, with all the ensuing responsibilities. I ended up living with Mum and Dad during the time that Peter was away. I was very conscious of the fact that he was missing so much of Andrew's growing up. I knew that this was a unique time in all of our lives, which could never be recaptured. So I bought a Polaroid camera, and used to send Peter photos of Andrew once a week, enabling him to chart his son's progress from afar.

After Peter returned from Belize we seemed to be forever moving from Germany to the United Kingdom and back again. Laura was born two and a half years after Andrew, and in the same hospital in spite of the fact that we lived in five different homes over a period of ten years!

It was lovely to have a tiny baby to look after again, and the birth of Laura delighted us all. Both Peter and I loved children and wanted more after Laura was born, but after experiencing the emptiness and sorrow of two miscarriages we knew this was not to be. The sadness that we experienced made us feel even more grateful that we had two healthy children, whom we loved deeply.

Peter was fairly keen to discover some spiritual life wherever we were posted, and so we all used to go along to the Anglican church service on whichever camp we happened to be stationed at. I have to admit that more often than not during the service I would find my mind wandering to what I needed to do to get the lunch on the table once we got home, or trying to remember whether or not I had turned off the hob before leaving the house, rather than concentrating on the content of the sermon. During the week Peter would attend a Bible study, making friends with the other members of the group, but I was content, if not relieved, to stay at home and look after the children. On the rare occasions when I did attend, I felt uncomfortable and way out of my depth with most of what was said and done. I tried not to get too concerned about my lack of knowledge and confidence concerning spiritual things.

What was I worrying about anyway? I attended church on a Sunday and had been confirmed, so I was a Christian . . . wasn't I?

I loved looking after my own children and, although I missed family and friends in England, decided to enjoy Münster in Germany as much as I could. We had been there for three years, and I knew that in twelve months' time we would be returning to the UK in order for Peter to take up a job with a gunnery school. But this was the army, and I was quickly to discover how soon well-ordered plans can change.

One morning, as I was getting on with my housework, I thought I heard a noise coming from the hall. The loud mechanical sound of my vacuum cleaner almost drowned out the insistent tones of the telephone as it waited impatiently to be answered. Turning off the noisy machine, grateful for a moment's peace, I was surprised to hear Peter's excited voice on the other end of the line. Although we loved each other, he didn't normally phone me at ten o'clock in the morning! He just said that he was coming home immediately as we had things to talk about.

Soon he was marching up the path, and announcing that he had been offered a posting to Kuwait, which would bring with it early promotion for him. The posting was the 'accompanied' variety, which meant that he could take us all along too. 'And we have till lunchtime to make up our minds,' he said when he had given me the brief details. Two hours to make such a big decision: we did what we normally do in times of decision: we sat down and had a cup of tea! Trying to think it through as logically as we could, we looked at the proposal from all angles, wanting to do what was best for us all. But as we chatted I was looking at Peter, with all the hopes and promise of an early promotion sparkling in his eyes, and I knew there was really only one decision that we could make. Having weighed up all the pros and cons we decided to go for it.

As with all decisions that are made in life, it pleases some and disappoints others. My parents were looking forward to us moving to the gunnery school, just a hour's drive from their house, which would have given them much more time with their grandchildren. They were naturally disappointed, and told us so. When I heard of their reaction, I felt doubts coming into my mind about our hasty decision, especially when I learnt that Mum was suffering from angina, causing her to get short of breath. But it was too late to reconsider by the time that news came through. We had signed all the relevant papers, and soon we would be on our way. So that was how, in 1988, we found ourselves, with some trepidation, setting off to our new home in a very different country and culture.

Disembarking from the aircraft and going into the airport of that desert country was like stepping into a tumble-drier – extremely hot and humid! The temperature on our arrival was 45°C – and rising – and it took us all a long time to acclimatise. The long sunny summers of my childhood in no way prepared me for this oven-like heat. The simplest tasks in those extreme temperatures became a huge challenge. Peter coped better than I or the two children did, as was proved in a rather embarrassing way when we first arrived. During our first week, while standing in a queue with some thirty Arab people awaiting some mandatory blood tests, I passed out! This caused quite a stir among the people who also stood in line, especially when Andrew decided to pass out in sympathy! Peter started to shout for a doctor, the woman who had been taking the blood samples kept repeating that she *was* a doctor, and Laura stood there, totally embarrassed by all of us. But the Bible states that all things work together for good, and we were to discover the truth of that verse, as suddenly the Barlow family found themselves at the head of the queue, with all the paperwork and blood tests completed in no more than ten minutes! This for Kuwait, with all its endless red tape, was pretty impressive.

Our first home in this unfamiliar country was a sixth-floor flat in Salmia, which was close to the city. Although very comfortable, its big disadvantage was the restriction it placed upon the children. They couldn't play outside because it was not safe for them to do so unsupervised, and in any case with temperatures rarely below 40°C, the air-conditioned flat was the only comfortable place to be, even for playing.

Kuwait has a culture quite unlike any Peter or I had ever experienced before. It was not just the heat that we had to get used to. It seemed at first as though everything was different – the food, the smells, the architecture – everything. Even the Islamic 'weekend' was on a Thursday and Friday, which seemed strange. And due to the incredible heat, all shops closed between noon and four o'clock for 'siesta' time. There seemed to be hundreds of mosques but only one Anglican and one Roman Catholic church in the whole of Kuwait. We started to attend the weekly Sunday evening service at the Anglican church, which for me was much the same as the other Anglican church services that we had been to. People are allowed to worship as Christians in that country only under sufferance and on the condition that Christianity is not discussed with the Arab community.

Although the Anglican church wasn't that different from what we had been used to in other countries, we soon found that the Islamic culture was very different from the Western culture that we had temporarily left behind. Arab men usually have at least two wives, and Peter was frequently exhorted to take another wife in order to have more children!

Arab women, who are looked upon as second-class citizens, are expected to walk with the children a few steps behind the men. In their houses, the men use the best room to entertain their guests while the women stay out of sight in a back room.

Other customs seemed odd to us at first: for instance, the Arab men would greet each other with a kiss on both cheeks, but if a man kissed his wife in the street it would be frowned upon and he would be liable to be arrested! Also two Arab men who were good friends would walk hand in hand down the street, but I found that if I held Peter's hand in public, it was thought shameful! I would often have a chuckle to myself as Peter had to resist the impulse to back off when an Arab male, known through his work, approached, kissed him on both cheeks and then held his hand! To resist would have caused great offence.

Because of all the influences that have come in from Western films, many Arab men would interpret the things that Western women did and wore as a sign of immorality, and I sometimes felt very uncomfortable when I realised that Arab men's eyes were watching my every move or when I realised that I was being followed; on other occasions, Arab men would bump into Western women on purpose. All of this was very unpleasant. My way of coping was mainly not to go out on my own, but even these things one got used to after a while, even though they never became acceptable or 'normal'.

Most Kuwaiti women wear black clothing that reaches from head to foot, leaving just a small open slit through which can be seen beautiful brown eyes. Older women would often spit at us, as they were aware how Western culture is encroaching on their own, and influencing their younger women, who were fighting for some recognition against the traditional lifestyle imposed upon them by

Islam. Only in the past few years have Kuwaiti girls had the right to education and women been allowed to work. Previously only boys attended school, and young women stayed at home to learn how to be good wives and mothers!

All that said, we enjoyed our time in Kuwait. It was a wonderful experience to live in so different a country to Britain and to be surrounded by such a contrasting culture. Even the more negative points of life were enriching in their own way, like dealing with the constant ingress of sand into one's ears, mouth and hair. What a pleasure to have a shower and feel cool and clean again – for five minutes! But even showering had its complications. The cold-water tank was situated on the roof, so it got the full effect of the summer sun. Thus the hottest water, which could seriously scald you, came from the cold tap, while the cooler water came from the hot tap!

Shopping in Kuwait was quite an experience. The local shops were only about half a mile away, and yet we hardly ever walked there, because it was far too hot. The shops were tiny, and the people who ran them didn't speak English, so I would wade in with my pidgin Kuwaiti and, with much waving of the arms and pointing to the things that I could see, managed to get by! Added to the language problem was the fact that one was expected to haggle for everything – it was just not done to pay the price first asked for.

The variety of food that we could buy locally was quite good. We had a butcher, a very good baker's shop selling delicious freshly baked bread, a fish market, which was a bit smelly but a place of fascination to Andrew, and a fruit market where things like fresh melons could be purchased. Outside the fish market were people sitting cross-legged on the pavement, selling tiny birds such as sparrows for the locals to take home and cook. Being English, of course I never even thought of buying them, and my only reason for doing so would have been in order to set them free!

My children became quite expert in bartering! Having very fair hair, which Arabs believe is lucky, Andrew and Laura were frequently followed so that their hair could be stroked in the belief that some of the 'luck' would rub off, a practice I never got used to and upon which I kept a very close watch! There were also supermarkets where the goods were of a fixed price albeit quite expensive. I felt safe doing my shopping in these places as they were very westernised and were usually patronised by equal numbers of Europeans and Arabs. Safeways took on a new meaning for me – it was the safe way to shop!

A few months after arriving in Kuwait we were transferred to the compound built specifically for the British Forces personnel. Although the houses were not of such a high quality as the city flats, the compound was the popular place to be among the expatriate community. We enjoyed life there with all it had to offer, including privacy from the local Arab population. Here we could relax, away from prying eyes. I knew that I could wear shorts in public and that I could swim in the sea without having to go in fully clothed, as was demanded on the public beaches, unlike the men, who could swim in trunks without incurring the wrath or attention of the local population.

But how quickly our little world was changing again now that Kuwait had been invaded. As I thought about the events that had brought us to this point, I peered through a crack in the curtains, trying to make out what was going on outside and what I should do next. Had Mum's angina and the feelings of hesitancy that I had about coming to Kuwait been a warning that we shouldn't have come, I thought, as I moved away from the window. No, I reasoned, that was silly. We had made a decision, weighed up the pros and cons and decided this was the next right move for us all as a family. How I wished Peter was with me now. But, for the time being at least, all the decisions were going to have to be mine.

I began to realise afresh how much I had relied on Peter's quiet strength and perpetual optimism. I tried not to panic at the thought of having to make all the decisions for us for the foreseeable future. Mentally and physically exhausted, I felt low, dejected and very vulnerable, with my morale at rock bottom as my mind dwelt upon the situation that I found myself in. As I sat slumped on the sofa, trying to decide what to do next, I felt a wave of emotion come over me, and I broke down and wept. As the hot salty tears coursed down my face, I realised after a while that this was not a luxury I could afford at this moment and, surprising myself, I began to pray, in spite of the fact that my previous prayer life had been restricted to following the prayers in a book in church.

The prayer, unpremeditated as it was, seemed to give me a sense of calm which allowed me to think a little clearer. I knew that I had to get my act together for the sake of the children if nothing else. With one parent captured, I owed them at least all the security and stability I could muster. I knew that if necessary I would be prepared to protect them with my life. Although that would normally sound over-dramatic, I knew that I was living through dramatic times. From that moment I went into 'automatic survival mode' and began to take up the responsibilities that now fell on me.

Still calmed by the prayer, I began to think positively about what I could do to improve the situation that I and my little family found ourselves in. Trying to put out of my mind any negative thoughts I had concerning Peter's plight, I weighed up the situation. I knew the only feasible way of communicating with my neighbours, because of the layout of the houses, was via the telephone. Picking up the phone I heard the comforting if somewhat shaky voice of Jackie, who was naturally feeling vulnerable. I knew Jackie to be a fairly strong character, who would put a brave face on things. Like me, she was alone in her house with her small children.

Jackie had used the time since Gerry was taken to ring around her friends on the camp, and found the same depressing news coming from them all. Their men had been taken, and they found themselves fearful and confused as to what to do next. But Jackie had more worrying news, which she held back from telling me immediately. Iraqi soldiers had already tried to force entry into some of the houses – unsuccessfully, but it was only going to be a matter of time before they succeeded. As she told me this, I felt the panic start to rise again.

Jackie meanwhile was giving me more information which made the immediate future seem more hopeful. 'Some of the women have left their homes and are starting to gather together for safety. Would you be interested in going to one of my friend's houses with your children, to save you being on your own, Sheila?' she asked kindly. Would I ever! Jackie agreed to phone around and let me know what would be possible. Within half an hour the phone was ringing again. It was Jackie, to say that some women were gathering at Linda's house and we were invited to go across and join them.

She didn't have to ask twice! I hastily grabbed an old sports bag and pushed in a few items of clothing, the photos I had for Martin and Vicki, and some documents that I thought might be of importance. What else should I take, I wondered frantically. I couldn't bear to leave behind one or two pieces of personal jewellery, which I ended up pushing into my sock in case my handbag should be taken from me. Waking my confused children, who allowed me to dress them in their half-sleep, I took a quick look around the room before hurrying into the inky darkness.

Jackie was waiting for us, just on the other side of her kitchen door. The harsh light from the bulb in the ceiling seemed to pick out the tension in her face, her short dark brown hair shining in the electric glow. Her face relaxed into a smile when she saw me with all my bits and pieces, and the children looking half asleep. Without wasting any time, we locked the door on Jackie's house, and started to make our way to Linda's. What no one had bothered to tell us was that a curfew had been instated on the camp, forbidding anyone from moving around outside after dark. Some soldiers who were guarding the entrance to the camp spotted us scurrying across the road, pointed their guns at us and began shouting in Arabic. Instead of trying to explain what we were doing, panic set in and we just ran all the faster! Luckily they obviously thought we posed no threat, and much to our relief the next few moments found us in the safety of Linda's house, among friends and not having to face the perils of the dark alone any more.

I looked around the room, and realised that being alone was going to be the least of my worries. The room was packed with familiar faces, women who, like me, had had their menfolk taken from them. Children seemed to be everywhere, some holding on to their mums for comfort, others talking quietly to each other, while still others had given up the battle against tiredness and fallen asleep on the floor. Linda, a fairly tall woman, slim built, with a strong personality, gave us a big hug and made us feel welcome. She had no more news to tell us, but said that she had a friend in the city who was keeping her updated by phone.

Right on cue the phone rang. It was her friend with important news. We strained to hear what was being said, but with so many people in the room we didn't have a chance of overhearing. It didn't matter, as Linda let us know exactly what had been said as soon as the call was over.

'It seems that the men were taken to a Kuwaiti police station, which the Iraqis have turned into their headquarters,' she said, looking slightly flushed. 'They were interrogated – but not tortured,' she added quickly, answering everyone's unasked question. 'They are all safe, and are now being transported to Baghdad. The British Embassy know what's going on, and are monitoring the situation very carefully. Colonel Duncan reckons that talks could even be under way right now to secure their release. That's about the top and bottom of it,' she concluded.

A general babble of noise broke out as soon as she had finished speaking as everyone tried to reassure each other or pick up points that they didn't quite hear properly. I found my mind racing. I was comforted by the news that our men were safe, of course, but why were they being taken to Baghdad, the heart of Iraq, instead of back to us, their families? I again found myself silently praying, this time for Peter and the others. We at least knew that they were all still alive, which was a lot to be grateful for. Meanwhile, the next obvious thing to do was to try and get some rest. Something told me that we were going to need all our wits about us during the next few days. Events ultimately proved that I was right.

4

The Will to Survive

Soon a new day dawned. Although it was great to be surrounded by friends, we all knew that we were now seriously overcrowded, and some new arrangements would have to be made, if only to make catering demands more manageable.

A couple of hasty enquiries confirmed that there was more space in a house nearby, where Pauline lived. So, after a hurried breakfast, the children and I made our way to her home, where Pauline and her three children welcomed us in. Several other women and their children arrived shortly afterwards, including Jackie, who was looking after a teenager who happened to be visiting when the invasion took place. But Jackie had the heartache of being separated from Colin, her nine-year-old son, who was visiting another family when the invasion happened.

Jackie was one of the few women I knew reasonably well before the invasion occurred. We had worked together for a while as helpers at the camp youth club, and had enjoyed our times together. Full of life, she was a great encourager, and I admired the practical way she got on and made the best of things, in spite of the pressures she obviously must have felt.

Knowing that Pauline's house did not have a phone,

I wondered how we would keep in touch with the other houses. What was devised was quite inventive. Needing to maintain contact with the next-door house, which *was* on the phone, we discovered that we could make ourselves heard by removing a polystyrene ceiling tile in both houses and then shouting through the gap we had made, making sure that we banged on the wall first! And we soon found that if we put a chair on top of the kitchen table and stood on that, we could hear and be heard even better! Working out the mechanics of all this raised a few smiles and relieved some of the tension we all naturally felt.

Looking around the room I noticed another lady, Sheila, sitting in a corner looking concerned, and supposed that worry about her husband was getting to her. But it turned out that it was the possible fate of her pet canary which was causing her anxiety, leaving it as she had in its cage in a now empty house. After a brief chat I agreed to go back with her to see what could be done. In the end Sheila decided to let it go, watching it fly into the bright blue sky where it would have a sporting chance of fending for itself. We heard later of a lady who, under great duress, had strangled her own cat rather than let it suffer at the hands of the Iraqi soldiers.

The World Service of the BBC came into its own for us all, as we tuned in each hour on our short-wave radio for the latest developments. The fact that they were broadcasting about our situation meant that the outside world was aware of what was happening in Kuwait and was monitoring the situation, which gave us great comfort. One report stated that 'some military personnel have been detained' and we knew that was a reference to our husbands. What they didn't say, of course, was that they had been seized by force from their families, who were now in fear of their own lives! Another report stated that the Americans, along

33

with other Allied troops, were on their way to Saudi Arabia. A further news bulletin which said that the American air force was already flying over parts of Kuwait was not as comforting as it may sound, as we knew that the oil refinery was now firmly in the hands of Iraq, and that if there were any reprisals we would be in the thick of it.

In spite of our fears, not much was talked about while the children were around, in case they picked up the negative feelings we had about the situation we were in, but we certainly made up for it when the last one was finally tucked up in bed. Hour upon hour was spent speculating on what the future might hold, before nervous exhaustion and fatigue got the better of us and we fell asleep on our makeshift beds on the floor.

At 5.00 a.m. I awoke, needing to visit the loo after all those endless cups of tea. I walked to the bathroom, and closed the door. Suddenly I became horrifyingly aware that I wasn't on my own! Hearing a slight noise above my head I looked up and to my horror saw two deeply tanned, hairy arms outstretched in my direction through a gap in the fan. I suddenly found myself overcome with a feeling of terror, which caused me to freeze like a waxworks dummy. The situation must have lasted only moments, but it was as though time stood horribly still, and everything was played out in graphic detail – the faded green of the Iraqi army uniform, brown arms reaching out for me, the persistent but gentle dripping of a tap that someone had failed to turn off properly making it all seem surreal and bizarre.

Suddenly the moment was past, and I saw his arms disappearing and heard the echoing sounds of fleeing footsteps. I wanted to leave that place immediately and tell the others what had happened, but found that I couldn't. I sat there for a few moments, trying to get over the shock that I felt, before rushing back and, in a panic but with a low voice so as not to wake the children, told the group what had happened. Someone suggested that we ought to go round and check the security of all the windows and doors, which we did, apprehensive about what we might find but glad that we could at least do something to make us all feel safer. I could have little inkling at this stage of the severe repercussions that this incident would have on me at a much later date.

Further sleep was impossible after this ordeal, but we all made an attempt at resting again, as we had no idea what new situations we would have to face when the new day arrived

We didn't have long to wait before the first incident of the day occurred. Just as we were finishing a simple breakfast of tea and toast, we heard a car revving up its engine, then at great speed racing around our camp compound. At first we could only guess what was happening as we kept all the curtains in the house drawn, so that we couldn't be observed by the Iraqi soldiers. Peering through a crack in the curtains, we could see what the noise was all about. The soldiers had hot-wired several cars belonging to families on the camp and were roaring around the area in front of our house, racing each other in a crazy, foolhardy way.

Whether they expected some kind of reaction from us I don't know, but they soon tired of this game and started to use the cars as one would bumper-cars at a fairground – but with a difference. Instead of bumping each other's cars, they changed the rules so that they smashed into trees and buildings, all of which was accompanied by loud blaring of the car horns, and much shouting and laughing. It was obviously all done for our benefit, as it was played out right outside our house, and whether we were supposed to be impressed or scared I will never know. Neither will I ever understand how they didn't manage to kill themselves. What they did do quite effectively was totally wreck many of the cars, while others were deliberately destroyed if the soldiers found that they couldn't be hot-wired. Many other vehicles were stolen and taken from the camp, and any valuables looted before they were eventually abandoned. Witnessing all these events sent our low morale diving even deeper, as it was obvious that there was very little discipline being asserted among the troops.

The heightened activity around us made us feel increasingly edgy. Gunfire rang out constantly, the occasional tank missile could be heard finding its target as it hit with a thump, then smoke could be seen billowing black into the air a few miles away. The older children in the house seemed to be coping with the situation really well, and they no longer asked to go out and play, seeming to be content instead to watch videos. It was the younger ones that I felt concerned for. They were harder to keep entertained, and couldn't understand why they were suddenly not allowed to keep to their normal daily routine. Having spent so much time with children in the past, I knew what a disruption that would be for them.

But a far more urgent problem confronted us. It was now impossible for us to leave the house, never mind the camp, and yet we needed fresh food which could still be purchased from the local market, in the form of bread, milk and fruit. God very often has the most unusual ways of answering prayer, but seldom could he have used a more surprising answer than the one in the shape of Hamoud!

Hamoud was an Arab from the Yemen, and had been employed by the British military to do plumbing and other odd jobs. He lived in a small house with his wife and children just inside the gates of our camp. I had always looked upon him as very much of a mixed blessing, given his previous track record. He would do a job, but left many others in his wake. I remember the day he came to fix the shower, which he did well enough, but after he had gone it took me ages to scrub the thick grease which he had managed to smear on the walls, the bath and the ceiling!

But now I saw him in a new light. Because he was an Arab he was still able to move around freely, and he offered to go and buy from the market all that we required for ourselves and the children. We would give him the money, and a little while later he would return, laden with all the things that we needed. And along with the provisions, he brought something equally precious – news of what was happening beyond our increasingly isolated world.

The very first time that he went shopping for us, we were all eager to learn as much as we could about what was happening generally. After we had patiently waited for a few moments while he quenched his thirst with the cold drink we gave him, Jackie said, slowly and deliberately, 'Hamoud, what did you see when you went back and forth to the market?' He thought hard for a moment, obviously trying to work out in the awkward English language all that he wanted to say. Then, speaking in a slow and hesitant way he began to tell us what he had observed.

'There is a large gathering of soldiers and tanks nearby,' he said in his heavily accented voice, enjoying the rapt attention that we gave to his every word. 'Small fights are taking place, but for the most part things are quiet. Peoples like you, they stay indoors,' he said, making reference to the many Westerners trapped as we were. Then he politely returned the glass, thanked us profusely, and went back to his own family.

The trips that he made for us to the shops and back went on for the first ten days. Then he decided to leave, and return to the Yemen with his family. Even though he was an Arab, it was obvious that he was concerned about his own fate and that of his loved ones. We, of course, wished him well and told him that whatever he needed to make his journey more comfortable he was free to take. He told us with gratitude that someone from one of the other houses had offered him a car, as his own was very old and unlikely to stand up to the journey. As I watched him disappear down the path for the last time, I felt bad that I had been so annoyed about all the grease he had left in my bathroom! I had judged him unfairly, and felt sorry that I had. He had turned out to be a good friend, and I wished him well. After Hamoud left, nobody took his place, and we had to manage on the little food that we had left.

Another person who came to our aid during those first few days of fear and uncertainty was Colonel Bruce Duncan, with his wife Toni. Bruce was the commander of the British Liaison Team in Kuwait when hostilities broke out. When they discovered our plight, he and Toni started a series of phone calls which helped and encouraged us, but which put them both in considerable danger, as all our telephone conversations were monitored. Bruce and Toni showed a deep care for others, and their phone calls made a big impression on us all. By contrast, other officers and their wives made it clear that they did not want us to contact them as they tried to avoid detection. We couldn't blame them, we were all trying by the best means we knew how to stay out of range of the Iraqi soldiers' wrath, but the phone calls we received from the Duncans, who never made us feel as though we were making a fuss over nothing, cheered us no end.

The kettle was constantly on the boil for another cup of tea, which enabled us to sit and talk through the situation – there was little else to do. The women who smoked seemed to smoke non-stop, rather than rationing out their supplies, deciding to face any shortage when it occurred. While some dreaded the withdrawal symptoms of nicotine, I viewed a tea-bag shortage with equal dread!

The fourth day since the hostilities began brought no sign of help from the British Embassy. The Iraqis were now preventing everyone from entering or leaving the compound, making us feel alone and isolated in spite of constant assurances from the British Embassy that they were monitoring the situation.

Then, around midday, someone from the house next door started to knock on the wall, the signal that a message needed to be conveyed. Even with us all as quiet as mice and Pauline standing on the chair balanced on the table, we still could not make out what was being said, but there was an urgency in the voice which we knew we shouldn't ignore. Pauline shouted as loudly as she could that we wanted to speak with them outside, in order to hear properly what was being said. They in turn made it very clear that they didn't want to risk doing that, but we insisted – having no direct communication with the outside world was sapping our confidence. Suddenly the door of the adjoining house flew open and one of the women, called Gily, yelled at the top of her voice, 'They're coming to get you!' and then immediately slammed it behind her again.

We all stared at each other with looks of horror and confusion on our faces. Who was coming to get us, and for what reason? We quickly concluded that Iraqi soldiers were heading in our direction. It had sounded as though it was being said that Iraqi soldiers had broken into the end of the terraced house next door to Gily's but we could not be sure whether we had heard correctly or not.

Smoke was still billowing black in the nearby town. Vehicles could be clearly heard advancing in our general direction. Panic set in, and through the hole in the ceiling we declared our intention of joining Gily's household. This statement was not received with any enthusiasm by them, but nothing was going to deter us. Scooping up the children, we grabbed a few belongings, flung open the door of our house, smashed the wicker fence that separated the two properties, and in seconds were standing inside Gily's house, gasping for breath. And now that we were there, nothing was going to persuade us to return next door!

Our panicky, ill-thought-out actions had brought new problems in their wake. We were now in a three-bedroomed house containing seven women, two teenage boys, one teenage girl and seven other children, ranging in age from two to ten! Our situation seemed to be getting more confined and restricted all the time.

Iraqi soldiers had indeed broken into the house now adjoining the one we were in. After their repeated pounding on the door, the terrified women inside had very reluctantly opened it. Several Iraqi soldiers then barged in, demanding money and jewellery. Worse was to follow. One of the soldiers suddenly produced a knife, grabbed one of the women and held the knife to her throat, as the other women and children looked on, helpless to do anything. Snatching her necklace from around her neck, he then proceeded to shove her into one of the bedrooms. At that precise moment one of the other soldiers glanced at his watch, said something in Arabic and they made a hasty retreat. A prior appointment had saved the terrified woman from a terrible ordeal.

Up to this point we had been aware that the soldiers now occupying the camp were an undisciplined rabble. The burnt-out and smashed cars underlined that fact completely. But now we knew that they were also ruthless and very dangerous. In spite of the fact that this incident had left them traumatised and badly shaken, the women had had the presence of mind to realise that Gily's household should be warned immediately of what had transpired, especially as they thought the soldiers were heading in our direction. We looked at each other in dismay, hoping that someone knew what we should do next.

I knew the situation was pretty grim. We were a household full of defenceless women and children, scared out of our wits, and with not a clue as to what to do next. But what we did or didn't do within the next few minutes might mean the difference between our safety and a nasty encounter with the Iraqi soldiers. We needed to act fast. I knew that Peter would have known exactly what to do, but he couldn't help us now. Think, Sheila, think! There must be something that can be done to get us out of this danger!

5

The Siege Continues

As my eyes quickly scanned the area in which we stood, trying to think what to do, I suddenly became aware of the table standing solidly in the middle of the room. For a moment my mind went back to my childhood in England. Occasionally, when the weather was bleak and we couldn't play outside, we would make a 'camp' underneath the table, and play for hours. Could it be that this simple childhood game could come to our aid now?

Quickly I explained my idea to the others, and we hastily grabbed the table and some mattresses, making a form of shelter, unsure of how good it would be in hiding us from the penetrating eyes of the soldiers, or keeping us safe from any bullets that they might fire at us. Then, trying to look and sound as relaxed as we could, we coaxed the children into this makeshift hide. They thought our quickly made shelter was a great idea, and wanted to know if they could have a picnic in their new Wendy house! We swiftly got a few biscuits and a little water for them, and told them to keep very quiet.

Our actions had been taken not a moment too soon. Just as the last person managed to squeeze into the shelter, we heard soldiers banging on our door, and, when no one responded, attempting to open it. We all froze; I was sure that everyone including the Iraqi soldiers could hear my heart pounding. After what seemed like an eternity but must have only been a moment or two, we heard a yell and the soldiers moved on. But only as far as the next house, the one we had vacated less than an hour earlier!

As we crouched under the table and mattresses, trying to keep as silent as possible, we heard through the thin walls the commotion that was now going on in our newly vacated house. We could only imagine what they might be up to. I kept thinking about the hole in the ceiling, which until a short time ago had been a life-line, but was now a potential threat.

After a little while we heard the voices begin to die down, and a empty, poignant silence hung in the air. By this time the children were totally bored with keeping so quiet and were no longer content to remain under the table. One by one we crept out, listening hard for any sound which would indicate that soldiers were still around. For the time being the crisis seemed to be over.

Darkness falls quite early in Kuwait, and soon we were facing another tense night, jumping at the sight of each other's shadows. Our fears seemed to grow stronger as the light became weaker. No one could relax enough to sleep for any length of time. Several of us volunteered to keep watch for a certain amount of time, but I soon found that even when it was not my turn to keep watch, it was still impossible to sleep. I lay there in the darkness, thinking of what Peter and the other men might be doing, wondering what effect our situation was having on our children, and wondering how it would all turn out. Everyone understandably seemed to be living on the edge of their nerves. I tried to bury my head in my pillow, and put the concerns I had at the back of my mind. I needed to get some rest. Tomorrow was going to be another long day.

As it happened the next day brought with it good news. Through one of their sources the British Embassy had heard of the forced entry of some of the houses, which we were pleased about, if only to prove the point that we were in no way over-reacting! The British Embassy must have made known their displeasure to the Iraqis; although our captors were still adamant that they were not going to release us, they reluctantly allowed Mr Weston, the British Ambassador, to pay us a visit. He was accompanied by another British official and two senior Iraqi officers. A meeting was hastily called, and I and several others were invited to attend.

We began to feel optimistic as we walked along to the meeting. Surely the Iraqis would see how senseless it was to keep us cooped up in this country, and would allow us to return to England and home? As the meeting progressed, we gained the impression that it would only be a matter of time before we were all free again. As soon as we had a chance, we asked Mr Weston the latest news on our husbands. Were they being treated well? Which hotel were they held in? Had they enough to eat? Were the Embassy staff in contact? His answers, although reassuring, got a mixed reception from us all.

'Your husbands are quite safe,' he said, beaming round at us all. 'They are being well looked after in a hotel in Baghdad, and are able to enjoy all the comforts that the hotel guests have, including use of the swimming pool!'

'It's all right for some,' said Carolyn drily, and we all laughed nervously, glad to hear that they were well but envious of their conditions after what we had had to go through. We soon realised that we had in our midst the one man who could make these conditions better for us, and we told Mr Weston in no uncertain terms that we saw the Iraqi soldiers as a real threat to our safety. He

44

bravely put this point to them, and after a long discussion they agreed that a male member of the British Embassy staff would be allowed to stay on camp to safeguard our well-being. Pleased at progress on that front at least, we went back to our house, where the other women were waiting eagerly for all the news. We told them how the meeting had gone, and how we would soon have a man on camp, representing our interests.

Some of the tension that we had all felt over the last few days started to ease. Several of the women fussed over their children, playing a game or telling them a story. Others chatted together, enjoying a cigarette and wanting to hear again everything that was said at the meeting. The evening wore on, and people gradually drifted into their own corners, settled their children, washed their clothes or tried to grab a little rest.

I found a quiet spot, sat cross-legged on the floor, closed my eyes and silently talked to God. I remembered the peace I had felt as I prayed that short prayer when the situation seemed hopeless a few days before, and I wanted to pray again. I prayed for my children, who were coping so well with this strange new life that we had. As a mother, this was one of my major concerns. I knew that so far they had coped with the situation well, but how long would it be, I wondered, before they began to pick up on the inner fears that all the adults had? I prayed for Peter, with the news of his well-being giving me a fresh desire to ask for God's protection in his life. I then found myself praying for my parents. I had no way of knowing what they had heard about the situation in Kuwait, but knew they would be worried about me and the children.

Although my prayers were sincere and from the heart, they didn't last long. Prayer was a new experience for me, and I soon ran out of words to say. My silent petitions had been spotted, however; Jackie made a beeline for me, and after a few moments of small talk asked directly if I had been praying! When I admitted that I had, one by one it emerged that others had been doing the same. Virtually all of the women who were still awake, which was practically everyone, admitted that they had been praying too, even though they didn't know much about God, or whether or not He could hear them. It has been said that there are no atheists in a foxhole, and this seemed to be the case now. Even though we previously had no need for God, we now prayed because no one else could help. At this point at least we were prepared to admit that maybe God could help us all.

A new day dawned, and with it new pressures. As always it was extremely hot, and we had a growing fear that our drinking water would soon run out. We normally drank only bottled water, as the tap water came from a storage tank perched precariously on the roof. Every couple of months it was refilled from a local water tanker, but how much water now remained was unknown. We started to drink this water anyway, using it for tea and coffee, making sure that the kettle boiled for a good few minutes to kill any bugs.

Food was our other concern. Since Hamoud left we had had no new supplies, and although we had enough for the moment we all knew that our supplies would not last indefinitely. We came to the conclusion that we would have to start some kind of rationing, of both food and water. This was hard for the children to take on board – before the invasion we used to be almost forcing drink down them every so often to ward off dehydration, and now, suddenly, we were restricting the amount of liquid that they could have. As with all kids, the very thing that is deemed unobtainable becomes desirable, and the children began to ask constantly for a drink, which most of the time we had to deny them for fear of running out.

On the hour we would huddle round the radio and listen to the latest news from the World Service. After a while some of the women chose not to listen as what was being reported was far from comforting. The main message that was broadcast was how Allied troops were building up on the Saudi border with Kuwait, and the advice for all expats was to take extreme caution and lie low. We still had contact with the outside world through the telephone, and we learnt through our friends in the city that many atrocities were taking place. We were told of people being dragged from their houses screaming, of the widespread looting that was going on, which involved whole buildings being stripped from top to bottom. The items that were being taken were not just jewellery, electrical equipment and money, but ovens, wall tiles, flooring, air conditioners, taps, baths – and even kitchen sinks! Whole paved areas in the city were being torn up and removed. Kuwait was being plundered by Saddam, who wanted to take as much wealth from his old enemy as he could.

Even more disturbingly for us, we heard of one group of Iraqi soldiers who were holding some English women hostage, and were raping them at will. This obviously upset us all considerably, and although we reported it immediately to the authorities, they said that for the time being there was nothing that they could do. When we heard this response some of the women in our group broke down, weeping for our unknown fellow captives and for what might yet befall us. We felt so powerless to help them, or for that matter to help ourselves.

Tension takes its toll on different people in different ways. Some people wanted to be doing things all the time, while others found it nigh impossible even to make a cup of tea.

Occasionally tempers would flare for no apparent reason, other than the great strain we were all under. Living on a knife-edge for days on end means that sooner or later people are bound to get hurt! Our frustration was increased by the knowledge that at the very beginning of the invasion we had had the opportunity to escape.

Later that day, the promised male Embassy official arrived on the scene. None of us were prepared for the kind of man he turned out to be. If at the back of our minds we thought we would be getting a staid, conservative government official, we had to revise our thinking pretty quickly. He was in fact a very cheery, full-of-fun kind of person, and did all manner of things to try and rebuild our confidence and allay our fears. Sadly, most of us had been through too much to appreciate some of his more bizarre antics, all designed to make us laugh, like wearing old diving flippers around the house, with a completely straight face, as though this was his normal garb! His name was Donald, and he moved into the house next door to the one we had recently occupied. For the next little while, I suspected, life would be far from dull. I wasn't proved wrong!

Donald was a fairly beefy chap, and showed a good amount of courage. With a smile on his face, he would do what he could to be helpful in the best way he could. Aware that most of the women were scared of what might happen to them during the night-time hours, he would walk around the camp at night even though a curfew was in place, which made some of the women feel decidedly uneasy, even though he did it to try and reassure them. He also made it his business to visit every house on the camp occupied by women and children, giving each household encouragement and hope. He helped in practical areas too.

Soon after he arrived, I found him in the kitchen, joking around with one of the children and making them laugh.

I knew that it would soon be time to put a meal together again, but food supplies were running very low. I found myself pouring out our tale of woe to him, not really expecting him to come up with any solutions, but I was discounting his ingenuity. With a twinkle in his eye he said, 'Well, my dear, there's no reason why we can't play the Iraqis at their own game, and go on a looting party – for the food which belongs to us anyway!'

The more we thought it through, the more right it seemed. We were permitted to walk outside, within the camp, in the daylight hours, but up till now we hadn't wanted to do this as we felt threatened and menaced by the Iraqi soldiers who were constantly on the prowl. But maybe if we had our Official Protector with us, things would be OK. Soon Donald, with Jackie and me in tow, was on his way to the first of several abandoned houses that we would visit that day.

As it happened, it wasn't the first time I had ventured out of the house, on an expedition of this nature. I had bought Laura a fluffy toy cat a short time before the invasion, in preparation for her birthday a few weeks hence. In monetary terms it wasn't worth much, but I wanted her to have it, as a way of comforting her. As I stepped over the threshold of the house where I had left it, I felt physically repulsed by the disgusting stench that hit my nostrils. The Iraqi soldiers, acting more like animals than men, had urinated everywhere, and had spread excrement up most of the walls. The contents of the fridge and freezer had been thrown on to the kitchen floor, and now lay rotting in a discarded heap. The combined putrid smell of all these things was almost overwhelming.

If what I smelt offended my nose, what I saw equally offended my eyes. The whole house had been trashed, and nothing seemed to have been left intact. Smashed photo frames lay in a heap, like discarded litter. The carpet, which a few days previously had been spotless, was now completely hidden by heaps of clothing, smashed glass and upturned furniture. Then I spotted Laura's toy sitting all forlorn in a corner, but mercifully untouched. I gingerly took it, and put in under my arm before getting out of the house as fast as I could.

We soon arrived at the first house we wanted to investigate. It was the one that we had vacated just the day before. The door was ajar, and we entered cautiously, not sure whether anyone was home or not! When we had left, in much haste, we had forgotten to lock the door behind us. 'That must have been a nice surprise for our visitors,' said Donald grimly as we made our way to the kitchen. Our plan was to salvage some of the food from the fridge or freezer. But we were out of luck. All the food had been needlessly destroyed, as both doors had been left open, with some food thrown on the floor and the rest left to deteriorate in the heat. None of the contents of the fridge or freezer were safe to consume, and already there was a rancid smell.

We moved through the kitchen into the small passage that led to the lounge, first passing the bathroom and two of the three bedrooms. I glanced into the bathroom which looked more or less as we had left it. As we advanced further into the house a strong odour drifted along the passage, first of diesel oil, closely followed by the pungent smell of sweat mixed with urine and excrement just for good measure! Our ears strained for any small noise that would tell us we were not alone in this house. I felt my heart thumping loudly, and hoped that no one else could hear it. Donald inched along the passage, leading the way, his normally relaxed face tense and taut.

When we came to the lounge I saw my black leather

handbag tossed on the floor. In my haste to escape, I had left it on the dining-room table. Now its contents had been pilfered, including a favourite red pen that I had been given for work I had done for the Wives' Club Committee. Putting it down again, I decided that I no longer wanted the bag. I had no purse or possessions to fill it; it was just something else to worry about that wasn't necessary any more.

The lounge was filled with blankets and duvets, and had obviously been used as a dormitory by the Iraqis. One of the things that we needed was bedding, so with no second bidding we grabbed what seemed the cleanest, bunched it up and ran out of the door. We loaded Donald up with as much as he could carry, and he proceeded to take it next door where he gave it to the others to put in our present dwelling. We then scurried round the house like hamsters, gathering up all we thought we might need, while at the same time keeping an eye on the road in case we were discovered by returning troops. When we had got all that we felt we needed, we locked the door and returned to our friends next door.

Jackie and I took a breather before visiting two further houses, this time on our own. We felt like criminals as we very stealthily made our way over to these houses. How ironic that we were the ones feeling this way, while the Iraqi soldiers were more than happy to claim everything as theirs, when in fact nothing actually belonged to them. These houses were further away than the one we had started with, and I didn't relish the prospect of doing the same thing again. But we needed so many different things that we felt the other houses would yield. And we were right. We discovered fresh and frozen food, all still edible, as well as more bedding and other odds and ends, which we knew would add to our general comfort. As we moved through the houses at great speed grabbing toiletries, pharmaceuticals and toothbrushes, I felt like a frenzied housewife suffering from severe shopaholicism! We also eagerly pounced on some children's videos which we seized with delight, as the children were totally bored with the ones we had back home. It felt really scary, as we knew we might be discovered at any moment. We finally felt that we had recovered all that we could, and retreated once more to the safety of our refuge, exhausted from the stress and tension that our salvaging expedition had caused us.

6

Kuwait International, Here We Come

Donald noticed the tension that had built up during the days on end we had spent cooped up in the house together, and encouraged us all to sit in the shade at the back of the house. This made us all feel a lot better, even though we didn't stay out for long. Gily had long given up trying to keep the house to her normal clean and tidy standards.

'You know, some of the women in the other houses have let their kids draw on the walls, to keep them amused. What do you think about trying it here?' Donald said, in a whisper, so that the children wouldn't hear, in case it got a negative response from us. But we all thought it a great idea, and much to the children's delight we were soon handing them pencils and crayons and telling them to get to work!

At first they couldn't believe it. Andrew, who had been given a handful of crayons by one of the other women, came up to me and said, 'Mum, can I really draw on the wall?' Bending down, I said, 'Yes, darling, but only in this house, not in anyone else's,' fearing that it might set a trend for the rest of his childhood! And so they began, each child instantly transformed in their own mind into a famous artist. Very soon wonderful murals appeared here, there and everywhere. The walls were decorated with all kinds of pictures, along with their names, the names of their football teams, and anything else that they felt was important. One thing we were careful not to do was to allow them to write anything against the Iraqis which might have had repercussions later on.

Donald kept repeating his assurances that we probably would not be held for much longer, but he also suggested that while we were here we might as well have a bit more space. We looked at him with open mouths. What was this unpredictable man suggesting now? That we start a building programme? 'No, more like a demolition programme, actually!' he said in his clipped British accent. 'What I was thinking was, why don't we knock a hole in the wall there, and make this house and the house next door into one?'

It all sounded so feasible when he said it like that, and before we knew it he had left the house, returning a short time later carrying a pickaxe which he had purloined from goodness knows where. He then started to attack the wall with great gusto, making a lot of dust and noise, which we felt sure would bring the Iraqi soldiers running. We mounted a look-out, and if we saw troops coming in our direction we told Donald to down tools for a while. Progress was slow, and eventually he stopped, putting the pickaxe under the sofa ready for the next day.

The stillness of the night was interspersed with gunfire as the Iraqis randomly fired their guns into the air, like kids with a new but deadly toy. We kept the electric light on all night, even though it made sleep almost impossible, hoping this would keep away the soldiers who were looking for shelter or unoccupied houses to plunder. But we realised that to some troops looking for the spoils of war, which we knew included ourselves, it would indicate where we were. However, the night passed without incident and we all looked forward to a new day dawning. What a relief to see the sun rise, dispelling the darkness that had blanketed us with fear. Each new day brought with it new hope. Could it be that this day would be the one when our nightmare would end?

I heard the children begin to waken from their sleep, and got up to make their breakfast. We no longer just took care of our own children, but had collective responsibility for all the youngsters within the house. Andrew and Laura, along with a couple of other children, announced that they were hungry. I put a finger to my mouth, signalling them to be quiet, and tiptoed to the kitchen, creeping past Maureen and her teenage daughter who were sleeping in the passage on a couple of mattresses. I was already dressed, as the little sleep that I had managed was taken in my shirt and jeans. Switching on the electric kettle, I was joined by a sleepy-looking Jackie, who had come to help. Together we prepared breakfast for the ten children who suddenly appeared like magic from nowhere. Breakfast consisted of a bowl of cereal and a piece of fruit. Soon the food had disappeared, so we gave them a drink of squash along with a piece of apple and then sent them to get dressed.

Jackie and I sat listening to the World Service on the radio. Margaret Thatcher's distinctive voice came over the airwaves, talking of not giving in to Iraq's demands on Kuwait. Although I agreed with her sentiments that force was needed to regain Kuwait for its rightful owners, sitting in the middle of the war zone didn't make me feel quite as resolute as Mrs Thatcher! The news bulletin over, I went for a quick wash in the bathroom, by which time the whole house had started to wake up and another day had begun.

Donald appeared a little while later, looking slightly stiff from all his physical labours of the day before, but otherwise just as bouncy and optimistic as ever. He had every reason to be pleased. Glenn, one of the teenage boys in our house, had asked him if he could lend a hand with making the two households one. Glenn was just like most teenage lads – average build and height – but his helpful disposition and a desire to *do* something probably made him volunteer his help. Donald very quickly agreed. Looking somewhat relieved, he handed Glenn the pick, and giving him some quick tips he then went to see how the other households were faring.

Glenn soon found that he was making very slow progress doing it the way Donald had suggested, but that if he worked at chipping away the cement surrounding the bricks, headway was greatly increased. In a short space of time he was making real progress and was thoroughly enjoying himself. Within hours a small hole had appeared, and half an hour after that we could wave to the occupants in the next house. By the time Donald returned the hole was quite a good size, and working together for the next hour they produced a space big enough for a person to crawl through.

Finally the task was complete, and we found ourselves living in a house which now had six bedrooms, and was occupied by ten adults and fourteen children under the age of nineteen! We were all justly proud of what had been achieved and were looking forward to all the extra space that we could enjoy. But our joy was short-lived. The dust had hardly settled from the last brick being extracted when word came that we should be prepared to move camp in half an hour's time!

Although we felt naturally frustrated at all that hard work for nothing, our thoughts were now concentrated on leaving the camp and, we hoped, seeing our husbands very soon. The few spare clothes and personal items, along with our shoes, had been lined up near the front door for days, ready to be snatched at a moment's notice, so we were all very quickly ready to leave.

The question was, did we have enough usable cars to get us to Kuwait City? My car was only twenty yards away. I had seen several Iraqi soldiers around it a few days earlier, trying but failing to get it started. Then they had come to the house, demanding that I hand over the keys. I had lied, denying that I still had them, trying to look fierce, but trembling inside. I knew that if they had been a little more insistent I would have cracked, but as it was they lost interest very quickly and lumbered off, looking for other pickings My car was now our escape vehicle, so I prayed that it had not been immobilised and that it would start. Thankfully, following a jump start for a flat battery the engine leapt into life. The car was soon packed with women and children, and we left the camp for the last time.

As we passed through the camp gates I began to realise how surrounded by the Iraqis we had been. Just outside the gates, sitting on a pile of sand and perched precariously at an angle, was an Iraqi tank. To the right, down the beach, were what seemed like hundreds of Iraqi soldiers dug into trenches. Along with these soldiers were anti-aircraft guns and other military vehicles. As we slowly drove down the small road that led to the fish market we passed yet more tanks and soldiers.

Although I had known that we were isolated in our houses, to see so many soldiers all preparing for war just filled me with horror, mixed with relief that we were now leaving all these things behind us. When we came to the end of this street a road block was pulled open to allow us exit. We drove on, through the marketplace, catching the curious stares of the scruffy, brown-faced soldiers as we went. They all looked as if fatigue and the extreme heat were getting the better of them as they lazily shifted their guns from one position to another.

We drove slowly as we passed through the deserted streets of Fahaheel Town. Cars with their windscreens shattered by bullets littered the roadside, some with their doors wide open, flapping in the wind. Other cars were crunched up against walls or lamp posts. The town resembled a ghost town, with not a person in sight. Some buildings had obviously come under attack and now stood forlornly, the hot sandy air penetrating their interior through the gaping holes.

Once through the town we quickened our pace, breaking all the speed limits in our haste to get to the Kuwait International Hotel, which was to be our penultimate destination before flying back to England from Kuwait City Airport. As we got nearer the city the roads became more and more congested with joy-riding Iraqi soldiers. These troops were a menace to themselves as well as to us. They raced alongside us, shouting and blaring their horns, cutting us up by screeching their brakes, swerving across our path and out again. We also saw truck-loads of looted possessions on the way to Iraq, along with many tanks rolling along, although thankfully on the other carriageway, going towards the Saudi border.

We played observation games with the children, asking them to count how many craters they could spot in the road, or the houses with the most holes in the side. The children all found this great fun, not for one moment realising the implications of what they were seeing. It never ceases to amaze me just how resilient children can be. God was truly answering my prayer for them. As I raced along the roads, trying to avoid the potholes and keeping a weather eye open for the next band of Iraqi soldiers, the kids egged me on with shouts of, 'Come on, Mum, we're winning!' thinking that I was trying to race the other cars. In truth, I was of course just anxious to get to our agreed destination in one piece.

After thirty minutes, which because of the hassle that we had experienced seemed much longer, we were in sight of the Kuwait International Hotel. Even with its top floor burnt out it was still a welcome sight, a place of beckoning safety. As one of Kuwait's luxury hotels, it was here we would wait until the arrangements could be finalised for us all to fly back to England. We had even been told that our husbands might have returned to England ahead of us. It was such a relief to know that within days we would be safely back home as a family. Scrambling out of the car, hot and dusty, we rushed into the lobby with our hearts pounding, our minds already anticipating a joyous reunion with our husbands in the very near future.

7

A Safe Haven

Apart from the top floor being destroyed, from the outside the Kuwait International Hotel looked fairly normal. But as soon as we entered the lobby of the hotel we realised that, like everything in a war situation, things are never quite what one would expect. So, instead of staff welcoming us to the hotel, offering to take our luggage and checking us into our rooms, we were immediately confronted by guards carrying kalashnikov rifles, and looking quite menacing. Unlike the soldiers we had left behind at our camp and the ones we had seen on our journey, who had been poorly dressed, with ill-fitting pieces of uniform and many of the soldiers wearing trainers on their feet, the men now confronting us were dressed very differently. Clothed in smart new uniforms, complete with black army boots, the contrast between them and those we encountered previously was immediately apparent. We were soon to learn that these soldiers were part of Saddam Hussein's highly trained élite troops.

We were shepherded past the soldiers as they guarded the entrance, and Andrew, with all the natural curiosity and bravado of a ten-year-old said to one of them as we were being herded past, 'Whose army are you with?' They spoke perfect English and answered, 'Iraq's.' Before

I could restrain him, Andrew responded with, 'Then you are our enemy.' I saw the muscles in the man's face tense, his eyes narrowing slightly. As quick as a flash I dragged my startled son away from the scene, at the same time muttering some nonsensical comments about the soldiers being our friends! Then, out of earshot of the guards, I sternly told Andrew to think before speaking and getting us into any more tight corners with his ill-chosen comments. Andrew couldn't see the point that I was trying to make. As far as he was concerned he was only speaking the truth, but, seeing that I was not happy with him, for the next little while he remained quiet.

Every few moments the revolving doors of the hotel would whirr into action, and more women and children who had driven their beaten-up cars into the hotel parking lot would enter the plush lobby looking tired, apprehensive, but relieved to have arrived at this so-called 'safe haven'. Before long, thirty-one women and over fifty children stood in the lobby, wondering what was going to happen next. A few tears were shed as Jackie was at last reunited with her son, whom she had not seen since the conflict began. I was also grateful to see once again friends like Nicky and Elaine who I had not been able to contact since the nightmare had begun two weeks before. Our exchange of news was short-lived, however, as a member of the British Embassy staff told us to gather round him, as he was going to explain to us what was to happen next.

He asked that we all hand over our passports to him, so that they could be kept safe and away from the prying eyes of the Iraqis. This was important as our passports declared that our husbands were serving British soldiers, a fact that we didn't exactly want to have broadcast everywhere! Then, speaking in a firm and unemotional way, he gave us as much news as he could.

'We would ask you all to remain in the hotel until such time as a plane is made available to fly you all back to England. We have been told that your husbands are safe in the Al Mansour Melia Hotel in Baghdad, and it is possible that they may even get home to England before you do,' he said, repeating a line we had heard before. He continued with other news.

'This hotel is also accommodating some top Iraqi army officers on what is now the top floor. It would be advisable not to speak or associate with them,' he added, and I half wondered if my young son's interaction had in some way reached his ears! He then requested that we try and keep the noise levels down, so as not to annoy the Iraqis. Then, after answering one or two general points, he was on his way, leaving us to chew over what we had just heard. We now began to understand why we had been brought to this hotel, and why there were so many guards positioned in the lobby and on every passageway. Having us living at the Kuwait International would add extra security for the Iraqis, as the Allies would be unlikely to attack the hotel with British women and children inside.

Soon it was the turn of the manager of the hotel to address us, giving us a warm welcome and saying how he and his staff would do their best to make us feel comfortable. He seemed genuinely sympathetic towards our plight, and expressed his hopes for a quick end to the situation. He then gave us a list of things we could do, as well as those things we should avoid, which included swimming in the hotel pool, as stray bullets from the conflict going on in the city had been found around the pool area.

After this briefing we were all checked into rooms. Andrew, Laura and I had a nice room on the third floor allocated to us, which was pleasantly furnished, the colours of the wallpaper and carpets giving it a calm, relaxing atmosphere. The room had just one double bed to share between us, and our own en-suite bathroom, the bath of which we had to keep filled with water in case of a fire.

As soon as the children had explored the bathroom and bounced up and down on the bed once or twice, they rushed to the window to see what kind of a view we had. From our room we could see the coastline, about seventy-five yards away. I was fascinated to see that the beach was a hive of activity, with some soldiers busily digging huge holes in the sand, while others put up tents. Then, as I strained my eyes to see clearly, I observed what looked like metal boxes, that it took two men to carry, being placed into some of the holes. I guessed that it was ammunition for their tanks and big guns that they had pointing out to sea.

I thought of Peter, and how he would be able to recognise and name all the equipment while to me they were just weapons of war. A lump came to my throat as I thought about him, and I wondered how long it would be before I would feel his comforting arms around me again. The question hung in my mind for a long time, with no answer forthcoming. I tried to enter into the excitement that the children felt about coming to the hotel with all its new things to explore, but deep down I knew that we were still in a very dangerous situation.

As the children started to unpack the few things we had been able to bring with us, I again peered out through a gap in the curtains, this time concentrating my attention on the coast road that lay between us and the beach. The road seemed to be fairly busy, as mainly light armoured cars and lorries hurried along it, with sometimes the occasional tank going about its grim business.

I knew that my best hope lay in being optimistic about our situation, and as I put away our few possessions, I began to think positively of all the things we now had going for us. We were miles away from the oil refinery which had been so close to our camp, we were able once again to relate freely with each other, without the restrictions of curfew, and maybe best of all, we had all the food we needed. In fact, as we were soon to discover, we were now presented with the best hotel food that we could wish for, three times a day! We ate the same meals as the Iraqi generals on the top floor; they had set mealtimes, and we would use the restaurant after they had finished. Not only were we presented with food of the highest standard, with at least three choices of main meals at most sittings, but we were waited on as if we were royalty!

Glancing at my watch I realised that it was time for us to go and have some lunch. As we left our room, I noticed to our left, at the end of the corridor, a soldier leaning against a wall. Instinctively we turned right and started towards the lift which was halfway along the corridor. A door creaked open two along from ours, and out walked Jean and her two children, Stephen and Helen. I had known Jean slightly ever since she first arrived with her husband and children at the camp we had just left. She was about the same height as me, with fair, neat hair. I knew her to be a quiet, thoughtful person, and was glad of her company. Her children were similar in age to mine. Stephen was a year older than Andrew and as time went on would prove to be of a rather serious disposition, possibly taking on some of the responsibilities as 'man of the house' while his dad was away. Helen was a few months older than Laura, with lovely blonde hair and a lighthearted, giggly personality.

We were soon all in the lift, heading down to the plush dining room, and we all enjoyed a lovely, relaxed meal together as we shared our stories, while the children made small talk mainly consisting of what they had chosen to eat and what they were going to choose next! Jean's experiences differed slightly from mine, as women had come to stay in her home, rather than her going to someone's home, as I had. When it was time for her to leave the camp, she had to walk out of her house, leaving many of her things behind, not knowing what would become of them all, which must have been hard.

I also discovered that Jean's household had knocked down a wall into the next house, just as we had, finding that a wooden partition was all that separated them, unlike the brick dividing our two houses. We laughed out loud at some of the things we had been called upon to experience, grateful for the absence of the intense fear that had filled every moment up until this point. We both concluded that neither of us were cut out to take centre stage in a war. Heroics were best left to heroes – not to homemakers!

The waiters were curious to know who we were and why we were staying at the hotel, and asked us many questions. They were also keen to glean any new information on what was happening around Kuwait. These hotel staff were originally from the Philippines or India, and, like us, were concerned that their families would be anxious for news of them, and handed us letters to post when we got a chance. Apart from us and the Iraqi army officers, there was another group of people staying at the hotel – businessmen who had been working in Kuwait when hostilities broke out, and who found themselves unable to leave the country. Bored and frustrated at not being able to get on with their lives, they were nevertheless extremely kind to us all, and especially so to the children.

Time passed quickly, and before we knew it the meal was finished and the children started to get restless, eager to explore the place. Their youthful enthusiasm rubbed off on Jean and me and we left the dining room in a happy frame of mind, ready to find out what our new 'home' had to offer. We were able to walk around the hotel quite freely, the Iraqi soldiers viewing us with mild curiosity. One of our first ports of call was the hotel shop which sold all the normal fare. I purchased a holdall for Andrew, a comic and crayoning book for them both, and one or two items of clothing, as the few items they now possessed were getting faded and worn.

The children soon discovered to their delight that the hotel had a bowling alley, tucked away at the back of the building. We went to investigate, and, finding it closed, vowed to return when it opened up. In the dim light we could just make out the pins gleaming white at the end of the alleys. Its discovery went a long way to compensate for the fact that the hotel swimming pool was out of bounds.

In spite of the enormous lunch that we had all eaten just a short while before, we all felt tempted to visit the hotel's coffee shop, where wonderful coffee, biscuits and cream cakes were on sale. As we all sat down to enjoy the food and drink, with the happy chatter of other families around us, it was difficult to grasp the reality of the situation we were in. Here I was, with my two children, experiencing with a friend and her two kids luxury that Peter and I could never normally afford, but in nightmare circumstances, which seemed part of a strange dream. I figured that the best way to cope was to just keep adapting to whatever circumstances we had to deal with.

After a while we said our goodbyes to Jean and her children, and went back to our room. Andrew and Laura turned on the television and discovered some cartoons that they were content to sit and watch. I lay on the bed, suddenly feeling exhausted, glad to be able to close my eyes for a while and rest. Sleep must have crept up on me, because before I knew where I was it was suppertime!

After a pleasant supper with Jean and her children I started to get ready for the manager's meeting, to be held late that evening. Discovering that most of the bedrooms had interlinking doors, we felt that it was going to be comparatively easy for a few of the teenagers to look after the younger children while we went to the meeting.

We soon found ourselves in one of the large rooms in the hotel, with the manager and his staff giving us as much helpful information as they could, and obviously wanting to make things as easy for us and our children as possible. He told us that the bowling alley would open once a day, and that he would arrange for a bouncy castle to be made available for the children before the evening meal so that they could let off a little steam before bedtime. He had even arranged for someone to come in and give the children judo lessons. He was obviously doing everything he could to make our stay pleasant. Some of what he had to tell us, though, was far from comforting.

'I am sorry to say that we have been getting reports of looters in operation in the town. In fact,' he said, his voice-level going softer with emotion, 'we have been told that one man has been hanged, publicly, as an example of what will happen to others who are caught. I think it would be best, therefore, if you stayed within the confines of the hotel.' After that grim news not many of us felt like straying far anyway.

It was agreed at the end of the gathering that a daily meeting be held to keep us informed of the latest developments. Instead of everyone having to go up to each meeting, a couple of women from each corridor were invited to go to the meeting and then report back to the others. I was not one of those elected to attend, and I started to feel left out, even though I knew that the women who did go would convey everything that I needed to know.

The meeting broke up, and we drifted back to our rooms, ready to thank our baby-sitters for their good work. What I discovered when I got back to my room, though, did not please me one little bit. Andrew and Laura had completely taken advantage of the fact that I was not around to keep them in order, and had got totally over-excited, jumping around and making lots of noise. Our poor baby-sitters, not much more than kids themselves, had not known what to do, and had let them get on with it! Pat, whose room was directly below ours, on returning from the meeting came up to see me, understandably angry about the noise, especially as we had been specifically asked to be quiet so as not to incur the wrath of the Iraqi High Command.

I apologised profusely to her, and after she had left turned to face my children. Suddenly, all the anger, frustration, tension and anxiety of the past few days seemed to well up in me, and I raised my hand towards Andrew with the intention of punching him in the face. I saw a mixed look of horror and fear in his eyes, and pulled back at the last moment, but he began to realise just how very cross I was with him and Laura. I then sat down and cried in front of them. This was a deliberate decision. Normally I saved my tears for when they were not around, but I felt they both needed to know some of the emotion that I was experiencing. That seemed to calm them down and clear the air, and that was the first and last time that I lost my temper with them, or that they saw me cry.

It wasn't the only time that Andrew had my mind spinning during our brief time at the hotel. Each corridor had a tea trolley on it, so that we could help ourselves to a drink when we wanted one. One sleepy afternoon, I asked Andrew if he would mind going to the tea trolley to get me a drink.

It was only when he had not reappeared after some time that I felt it was necessary to see what he was doing.

Opening the door of the room, to my horror I saw Andrew with a loaded rifle in his hands, passing the time of day with the Iraqi soldiers! Apart from the obvious dangers of the loaded rifle, we had been specifically told not to associate with the Iraqi soldiers, and I was as concerned that nobody witnessed the event as about the dangers from the weapon!

I said in a weak voice, 'Andrew, where's my tea?' and he passed the rifle back to the soldiers, picked up my drink and with a cheerful smile said, 'Here it is, Mum!'

'Well, let's take it inside,' I said, as I guided him back to our bedroom. Once inside I told him that it was *not* a good idea to speak with the Iraqi soldiers. He looked at me as if to say 'What's all the fuss about?' and flicked on the TV. I found that I was no longer feeling sleepy, and that I could have done with something slightly stronger than tea to drink!

Now we were in a comparatively safe place, with all creature comforts met, I found that the need that had been there up to this point to keep thinking positively and to keep my wits about me subsided, and, with lots of time on my hands, the reality of our situation began to sink in. I began to feel depressed and very low, wanting so much for the whole thing to be over, and wanting more than anything else to see Peter again. I felt like a bird in a gilded cage – food and drink provided, and yet still not free to do as I liked.

At each daily meeting it was said that we could expect a flight back to the UK any time, and in fact at one meeting everyone had been told to pack their bags and stand by for a middle-of-the-night departure from the hotel. I had been blissfully unaware of this order, and wondered why

when I went to the restaurant for breakfast the next
morning everyone but me and the children looked tired
out! Hopefully if a departure had taken place someone
would have come looking for us . . .

The Iraqi authorities then said that it was impossible to
find aircraft to fly us back to the UK, and that the only
other option was for us to join our husbands in Iraq. They
wanted to know what we thought about that. Realising
that this was probably our best option, we decided to agree
to their plan. The British Embassy attempted to arrange
buses to transport us, but these did not materialise and
we were asked if we would be willing to drive ourselves
there. We were so anxious by this time to see our loved
ones that we agreed, but another obstacle had first to be
overcome. Some of our cars, which had been parked in the
car park underneath the hotel, had been vandalised and
there were now not enough cars to get us there. However,
the British Embassy and friends from the city came to our
rescue, finding people in Kuwait who were willing to give
up their second car for us to use.

After an early breakfast, just seven days after we had
arrived we were leaving the hotel. The hotel staff had made
up packed lunches of chicken sandwiches, fruit, cake and
cheese, along with some bottled water. We shared my car
with Jean and her two children, and soon we were rolling
out of the hotel area, with soldiers from the Iraqi army
escorting us through war-torn Kuwait, with most of the
buildings, including the royal palace, looking decidedly
the worse for wear. Our first stop was the British Embassy
to pick up members of staff who would also escort us to
Baghdad. Surely it couldn't be too much longer now before
we were united as a family? As I waited for the convoy to
get started on the journey I kept thinking to myself, 'Hang
on, Peter, we'll be with you soon!'

8

The Road to Baghdad

As I waited with Jean and the children for the convoy to move off, I began thinking through all the things that I had recently experienced. I found it almost impossible to take in everything that had happened within the space of two weeks. For me, two months would have seemed a more reasonable estimate of time.

Many of the vehicles in the convoy had seen better days, and I wondered how they would all cope on the journey we were about to embark upon. I counted myself quite fortunate. The first car we purchased when we entered the country had let us down quite badly, until it broke down once too often and Peter had replaced it with the car which I was now driving. Even though it had Union Jack tape stuck along the top of the windscreen and along its sides I knew it was far more reliable than our previous one, which had been a liability.

My memories of the past were interrupted by the sight of an old man on a bike who suddenly came into view. As he drew closer I realised that he was selling ice creams and water from a container on his bike. Every cloud has a silver lining for somebody, and he obviously hoped that he would make a little money from selling what he guessed people setting off on a long journey might most want – a

71

cold treat and cool water. He spoke little English, and as he rode slowly down the lines of cars, he kept repeating the words 'ices, water' with a toothless grin on his face. Andrew had a few Kuwaiti coins which were burning a hole in his pocket, and I guessed what was coming next.

'Mum, can I buy some water from that man? I'm feeling so thirsty! I'll pay for it myself! *Please*, Mum.' There was no way that we needed any more water than we had already, but in order to keep him quiet, I allowed him to buy two small bottles. What harm could it do? Andrew was pleased and somewhat surprised that I had relented so quickly. He felt quite grown up as he pointed out the water bottles that he wanted and handed the few coins to the water vendor, who viewed the money with delight. The transaction over, the man went happily on his way, and the incident was soon forgotten. It would be many hours later before any of us realised how important that small incident would turn out to be.

Embassy staff were strategically placed between our cars so that all the women and children would have a male Embassy official not too far away should a problem arise. We had already worked out a scheme to alert each other should there be a reason for the convoy to stop. Using a system of flashing lights which would be picked up by all the other cars, we guessed that we could bring the whole convoy to a halt quite quickly. Explaining this briefly to the Embassy staff, I hoped they understood what we had been trying to say.

It was a odd journey that we had embarked upon, made up of a string of women and children, with a sprinkling of Embassy staff, being escorted along baking roads by Iraqi guards. How did I get involved in all this, I thought to myself as I glanced in the mirror at my hot and tired children, and then at my hair, which already looked as if it hadn't seen a comb in months! We went on for mile after mile, with the guards sometimes holding up the traffic at intersections for us to go through, much to the intense annoyance of the other road users who would blare their horns as we passed by.

After we had been going for a while we pulled up in a suburban area behind a block of flats. A wonderful aroma of freshly baked bread drifted into the car, as word went round that we had stopped to pick up some rations. Jean and I sat there with expectancy, wondering how much of the lovely-smelling bread we would be given. How we laughed when some Russian cars joined the back of the convoy. The rations turned out to be Russians!

Shortly after leaving Kuwait City the landscape became peppered with tanks and missile launchers, and evidence of skirmishes that had taken place in the not too distant past. All around us was sand and more sand, with one lone tree standing in defiance on the horizon, a statement that life can survive in the most hostile environments. What the landscape lacked in natural features it made up for in human form. The area was full of soldiers, who swarmed like ants everywhere, while their sandy camouflaged tanks sat awaiting orders to push south to Kuwait. The soldiers themselves looked a sorry bunch. Many seemed to be little more than boys, and my heart went out to them as they stood by their vehicles with empty tin cups in their hands, begging for water. I resisted the urge to give them any, as I knew if I gave to one, all the others would demand some too. Although they were just lads I knew that I couldn't fool myself into thinking that they were harmless. What a mess war is, I thought, making us all react contrary to our normal instincts.

We eventually reached Basra, the border town between Kuwait and Iraq, giving us a chance to eat and drink and stretch our legs. But we discovered that the food we had brought with us, which we had stored in the boot, was completely inedible, save for a few apples. We were also using more water than we had anticipated, and we had very little left. How I kicked myself for not letting Andrew buy all the water he wanted from that funny, toothless opportunist! But there was nothing for it but to make sure that we were careful about how much we drank from now on.

The journey continued with no hold-ups now that we were away from the busy traffic of Kuwait. We passed through many villages made up of little houses, many of which seemed in a bad state of disrepair. We saw women dressed in black, and poorly dressed children, but hardly any men, who I suppose were away fighting in the war.

Jean had brought a map with her, and every so often checked it to see if we really were being taken to Baghdad, as we had been told, or whether we were bound for another destination. A few days before setting out on this journey we had heard on the World Service that a man had been shot as he tried to escape across the border, so we knew that we had no option but to keep in the convoy. To do anything else would have been sheer folly. Occasionally we saw sandy-coloured tanks coming towards us, sometimes making us get off the road so that they could get past.

We had now been on the road for twelve hours, in intense heat, going through very boring landscape. The children had been marvellous, but they were starting to get over-tired, and little quarrels started to break out between them. Help was at hand, however, as one of the guards said that he had a relative living in the area, who he guessed would allow us to use her facilities before continuing. It crossed my mind how fortunate we were that the guards saw us as helpless women and children, not as the enemy of the Iraqi people.

I now looked on these guards as men with feelings who, like us, had just happened to get caught up in this war. He drove away from the convey and returned a short time later with a smile on his face to say his aunt was waiting for us in a nearby village.

Soon we were at her house which, like its occupant, was old and poor. But what warmth and love we received from this wonderful lady who did everything that she could to make us feel welcome and comfortable. At the beginning of the conflict, while still in the camp, we had been confronted by some of the worst type of Iraqis – the soldiers who had done some terrible things – but here, by contrast, was this lovely lady showing us that there are definitely two sides to every situation. Neither she nor her daughter spoke English, but their smiles and nods said more than words could ever do. Her toilet was a hole in the ground in a little shed at the end of her yard. She had little, but gave so much, her hospitality and cheerfulness warming our hearts as we shivered in the cold night air. Her daughter chipped away at a block of ice. When she had enough pieces they were boiled in a large pan on the stove. From this was made sweet, thick, Arabic tea, served hot in little glasses. The tea was not really to my taste, but I appreciated the care that went into making it. I will never forget that little oasis in the desert and the kindness shown to us by a stranger. I felt quite sad when it was time to leave her and rejoin the convoy.

When we were reunited with our friends we found out that Elaine's two small sons had become badly dehydrated, and needed medical attention urgently. The guards offered to take Elaine and her children quickly to a hospital in Baghdad. This they could do quite speedily if not hampered by the convoy, and Elaine and one of her friends agreed to go with them. I felt sorry for Elaine, usually a very fit, sporty lady with a cheery disposition. Now her suntanned face was pale and etched with concern for her children as she left us.

Fatigue was now taking its toll on all of us. I was fortunate because Jean and I shared the driving, but Glenda, for instance, had driven every inch on her own, and wearily said that she just didn't know how much longer she was going to be able to keep her eyes open.

The Iraqi guards saw the sense of what we were saying about getting rest, and said that they thought there was somewhere up ahead where we could have a break from the drive. So we all got back into our cars once again, now having to drive with our headlights on as the night was pitch black. After about another hour's drive, we arrived at what looked like a sports stadium, and we were told that we could rest here for about four hours. I looked at Andrew and Laura and Jean's two children, fast asleep, with their heads lolled forward or leaning on the next person's shoulder. What an ordeal for them, but at least, I reasoned, they were now resting for a while.

Jean tried to make herself as comfortable as possible in the passenger seat, but I couldn't get settled in the driver's seat as the steering wheel kept getting in my way. I decided to get out of the car for a while to stretch my legs, and in doing so woke Laura up. 'What's wrong, Mum?' she said sleepily. I told her that nothing was wrong, I was just having a break from sitting in the car. She also got out, without waking up the others, and we chatted for a few moments. Then I remembered that I had put an old tartan rug in the boot, so I got it out and laid it on the ground. Laura lay down on it and soon started to doze. I decided to lie next to her, only to realise that wild dogs were lurking just across the way! I'd read somewhere that they can sometimes attack humans, and although I knew that this was rare, it still prevented me from getting any sleep during our stop-over.

The journey continued, with just a short break to buy petrol, and water from children who I had spied just as we were about to speed off again. Our delight at finding someone willing to sell us water turned to despair when we realised that some of the water looked as though it had come straight out of the local pond. However, we agreed to buy some that looked reasonably clean; it cost us about as much as the petrol we had just filled up on!

Eventually we started to pick up road signs to Baghdad. Our spirits started to lift, even though we were so very tired now, because we knew we would be seeing our husbands within an hour! At the end of a very long road was a road block. We all pulled up as the soldiers wanted our passports, which of course we still didn't have. The Embassy staff, on the other hand, did have theirs, as well as diplomatic immunity, so we were moved to one side while the Embassy families were allowed to go on their way to Jordan and then home to Britain.

One Embassy man stayed behind to try and sort things out, but he was getting nowhere, as the soldiers wouldn't budge from their position that we weren't going any further without the right papers. It was eventually decided that the only way around this impasse was for him to leave us all where we were, while he went to Baghdad to get the necessary documentation for us to continue. By now the sun was high in the sky and the temperature must have been in the low fifties. We had been told before we started on the journey to 'dress down' so as not to look too glamorous when we arrived. Some fat chance of that, I thought. We had been on the road for over twenty-four hours, and were tired, sweaty and frazzled. We must have been the least alluring group of females that ever tried to enter Baghdad, making the Wicked Witch of the West look like a fabulous sex symbol!

Finally, after yet more hassle from soldiers demanding yet again that we produce our passports, the man from the Embassy arrived with wonderful news. 'I have the papers, and can tell you that your husbands are waiting for you in the hotel just down the road. Soon you will be able to put all the worries and pressures of the last two weeks behind you.'

Suddenly the tiredness and heat didn't seem so bad, as we took in this wonderful news. The convoy started up for the last time, and irritatingly we went the long route round, finally arriving at the hotel twenty-seven hours after we had started off from Kuwait.

The man from the Embassy said that he had been barred from entering the hotel so he couldn't escort us inside, but it didn't really matter as we would see our husbands there waiting for us. Thanking him, and our Iraqi guards profusely, we walked into the hotel, eager to see our loved ones again. Fate, however, had another surprise up its sleeve, which even the Embassy staff had not foreseen.

9

Where are our Husbands?

Entering the lobby of the Al-Mansour Melia Hotel we were immediately confronted by what had become the mandatory presence of Iraqi soldiers. We were all mentally and physically exhausted, but the adrenaline that was pumping through our bodies carried us forward. Wishing for once that I was slightly taller than five foot, I craned my neck to see past them for a first sight of Peter. But instead of the smiling faces of our husbands, it was the sullen faces of yet more Iraqi soldiers that caught my eye, indicating that they wanted us to go into the dining room that was to the right side of the lobby.

It was Jean who suddenly plucked up the courage to ask the question that was in all of our minds. In a clear voice edged with tension, she said, 'Where are our husbands?' No answer was forthcoming, just a shrug of the shoulders as one of the men muttered something in Arabic. I suddenly felt the atmosphere in our group change from excitement and anticipation to one of uncertainty. I couldn't put my finger on it, but I felt that something was wrong. Or was I just over-tense and over-tired? As I was trying to work out just what was going on, Elaine, who had left the convoy at great speed with some of the Iraqi guards to take her children to hospital, walked into the room with her husband, Michael, at her side. They were holding hands, but both looked decidedly strained.

I wondered if all was well with their children. 'Did they get to hospital in time?' I enquired.

'Yes, the guards were great,' said Elaine, with hardly a smile on her face. 'They rushed us through the traffic in double quick time, and they both received immediate medical attention for dehydration, so they're fine.'

So why are you looking so glum, I wondered, but felt I couldn't ask such a direct question. Then Dougie, Pat's husband, came in. Pat jumped to her feet, and with a little cry of relief flung herself in his arms. She had a positive, outgoing nature, even when dealing on her own with her teenage children. We looked on, grateful that these families had been united, but puzzled that there were still so many long faces. What on earth was going on?

Michael straightened himself up, obviously concerned about what he was about to say. 'Look, there is no easy way of telling you all this. I'm sorry but your husbands are not here!' He gripped Elaine's hand a little tighter as he said it, and I knew it had not been an easy thing for him to convey. Elaine looked down at the floor, almost in tears, and I sensed they felt bad about being together when the rest of us were still separated from our men.

We all looked at each other in a stunned silence of disbelief. How could this be true? Only a few moments earlier we had been told by the British Embassy that our menfolk were waiting for us in this very hotel. So what had gone wrong, what had suddenly changed? Pandemonium broke the silence as everyone started firing questions, all at the same time. Mike held his hand up to get everyone to stop talking and said, 'Quiet – please listen.' Once more the room was so silent you could have heard a pin drop. Tears were silently sliding down anxious faces, as all eyes were once again fixed on Michael. He carried on with his story.

'Last night a bus arrived and drove all the men away, apart from me and Dougie. Why they left us behind, I have no idea,' he said with a pained expression on his face. 'They wouldn't tell us where the fellas were being taken to, but they did say they would be unharmed. And that's all I know. I'm sorry.' The last words were hardly out of his mouth before women were rushing up to him, trying to find out a little more about their own menfolk.

Jean and I looked at each other, too tired and distraught to say or do anything but slump in chairs near the dining tables, with pristine white tablecloths and gleaming cutlery in readiness for the next meal. We were both trying to adjust to this new twist in our already complicated situation. I felt my eyes filling up with tears, which I tried to wipe away quickly with my sleeve. I wanted to be strong for my children, who were looking bewildered and confused. I felt I was always pushing down emotions that needed to surface, unaware of the emotional price I would pay later. Dougie came over, his sandy-coloured hair ruffled slightly by the greeting he had received. In his warm Scottish accent he said how uneasy he felt at being here when the rest of the men weren't. We tried to assure him that no one felt resentment at his or Michael's presence in the hotel, on the contrary we were pleased that they at least were safe.

The children were devastated at being unable to see their father. For the first time Andrew and Laura were filled with their own terrors. Laura pulled at my arm and asked, sobbing, 'When are we going to see Daddy?' I kissed her gently on the top of her head and answered her question as calmly as my shaking voice allowed. 'Soon, my love, I hope very soon.' Andrew was angry with the situation as he saw it. 'What have they done with him, why isn't he here?' he snapped. I hugged them both to me, smoothing their hair with the palm of my hand. Trying to sound optimistic, I said, 'Don't worry, he'll be all right. You know your dad's made of tough stuff. I'm just sorry he can't be here now.' As I said that I felt a lump coming in my throat, making it hard for me to swallow. I looked away from them both, before they saw my distress which would only serve to heighten their own.

I saw that one of the hotel staff was handing out room keys, and I broke away from the children for a moment to pick up two sets, one for us and one for Jean. I put a set in front of her, and not bothering to sit down again I gave her a quick smile and said, 'Jean, I think I'll go and find our room now. The kids are tired out, and I'd like to spend a little time alone with them.' Jean stood up from the table and nodded. 'That's what I need to do, too,' she said, scooping up the keys. 'Let's go and find our rooms together.' We trooped out of the dining room, which was gradually emptying as our convoy tried to come to terms with their new surroundings and this unexpected and unpleasant news.

Within a few moments we had made our way to the lifts which would take us to our rooms. Andrew rushed forward so that he could be the one to press the button to summon a lift down to the lobby, and within moments the indicator above the doors showed that one was on its way. The lift doors swished open to reveal an armed soldier who was doing the job of a lift attendant. As we entered the small enclosed space of the elevator his stale body odour was quite overpowering, and we were thankful when we reached the sixth floor and could get away from the foul smell. We stepped out into a small square area which had a few chairs around it, on which sprawled Iraqi soldiers. They scowled at us as we walked past, looking far from friendly.

Jean and I walked down the corridor, with our children trailing behind, and quickly found our rooms, which we were both pleased to realise were opposite each other.

I unlocked the bedroom door, long past caring what it might be like, just grateful that I had somewhere to rest, and to be able to shut the rest of the world out for a while. I was pleasantly surprised, therefore, to find that although the room was not quite as plush as the last one we had occupied, it was still of a good standard, with twin beds and an en-suite bathroom. From the bedroom window I could see the River Tigris glistening in the sunshine, with the bridge which spanned it carrying the bustling traffic from one side of the city to the other. Palm trees swayed gently in the breeze, and the scene was marred only by the anti-aircraft guns situated on the top of a mound of earth overlooking the bridge.

I sat down on one of the beds, and patted either side for the children to join me. Andrew and Laura flopped down at my side. My heart ached from all these new developments and my head felt very heavy. I was afraid to analyse the news I had heard concerning Peter. It was just too painful to contemplate what had happened to him and the others. 'Let's pray for your dad,' I said. Praying out loud was something I had never done outside a church until hostilities broke out around us at the beginning of August, but now I prayed with the children every night before they dropped off to sleep. Putting my arms around the children I closed my eyes. I prayed for Peter in simple language, partly because I wanted the children to understand what I was saying, and partly because that's the only way I knew how to pray! 'Dear God, please look after Andrew and Laura's dad. Keep him safe wherever he happens to be. Help us to be strong with whatever happens next, and please take care also of Andrew and Laura. Protect them from fear and harm. Help me to be a good mother, and be with us all. Amen.' That was it. My prayer contained so few words. Would they be enough? Yet I had felt a peace as I prayed. Help was what we all needed, and I hoped that my cry had been heard and would be answered.

We were all so exhausted that we sat on the bed for a while longer, not saying much but just glad that our mammoth journey was over and grateful of the chance to be on our own for a while. All too soon, though, it was time to make our way to the dining area for lunch. We soon discovered that we would not be permitted to walk around freely on our own any more. A guard would grant – or deny – permission for us to move from our rooms as he chose, and soldiers were posted at the lifts and stair areas, stopping free access. We met Jean with her two children on their way to get some food, so we got a table together to eat what was on offer. The children tucked in heartily, having not really eaten for a whole day. Jean and I ate a little, but had more pressing thoughts on our mind than food. We spoke together in hushed tones, not wanting our feelings to be heard by a wider audience. How could we have been so gullible as to trust the Iraqis, we asked ourselves. We would never again believe another single word they uttered. We felt sure that the British Embassy were convinced that we were now reunited with our husbands, so therefore the Embassy would not be too concerned for our welfare. They had been duped, and so had we. 'Where are our husbands?' I said to Jean in a whisper, knowing that she had no more clue than I did. Were they still alive? Did anyone know what was going on? Did anyone care?

The last question was unfair and full of self-pity, but this was how I felt. I wanted to feel positive and brave, but pessimistic and weak would have summed me up better! Glancing around the room at the other women and their anguished faces, I knew I was not alone with these feelings. Distressed I may have been, but I could not allow this situation to break me. My children were depending on my strength, and so I once again buried my true feelings and carried on as best I could.

The meal came to an end. Jean and I had just decided to make a move when the dining-room doors suddenly opened and three men dressed in lightweight suits walked quickly to the centre of the room. Everyone immediately fell silent, waiting expectantly for something to happen. One of the men began to speak in English, with a heavy Iraqi accent that was hard to understand.

'We need your names,' he said, 'so that you can be with your husbands, who are perfectly well. Please write your names on the list.'

'Where are our husbands?' many voices rang out in unison.

'They are safe, do not worry,' was the only reply he would give. Realising that we were not likely to get any more information from these men, who probably knew very little anyway, Jean and I added our names to the list before making our way to our rooms again.

The children needed no coaxing to go to bed; before I knew it they had slid between the sheets, Andrew at the head and Laura at the foot, and a few moments later they were both fast asleep. I smiled at them as they slept, crept over to where they lay and tenderly kissed them both, whispering to them how much I loved them. Within a very short space of time I was in the other bed totally exhausted from all the events of the last twenty-four hours.

Sleep is a great healer, and we all woke many hours later feeling much more cheerful and ready to cope with what the day might bring. Quickly getting dressed we left our room and joined the other women and children, many of whom had chosen to sit in the hotel corridor chatting rather than staying alone in their rooms. Laura and Andrew soon found friends that they could dash up and down the corridor with, while I exchanged news with as many as I could. I started to chat to Karen, who had been particularly kind to Laura when we shared one of the houses together, but our conversation was cut short as we became aware of something going on at the end of the corridor.

A couple of soldiers stood by the lifts, and one was reading something out from a piece of paper. A small group of women had gathered round to listen. He was in fact reading out a list of names, and Karen and I broke off our conversation in order to hear what was being said. We started to walk quickly up the corridor and caught up with Jean, who had already seen what was going on and was making her way over. Just on cue, as we got within earshot the three of us heard our names read out! He then said. 'If your name has been read out, prepare to leave the hotel. You will be going in your cars to meet with your husbands.' We established that just ten women and fifteen children were on the list. I didn't like the sound of it at all. Could we believe what the Iraqis said any more? Why were only some of us going, and not everyone? It was obvious that my misgivings were shared by others.

'Where are you sending us?' 'How far will we have to travel?' 'Do we need food and water?' The questions came thick and fast, with the soldiers looking more and more agitated the more we quizzed them. They were not used to women demanding answers to anything, as women in an Islamic society were supposed to be seen and not heard! But what was worse for them was that they did not have an answer to any of our questions. And without any answers we made it plain that we would not be going anywhere, so they reluctantly departed to report to their superiors.

The departure of the soldiers left us with an anti-climax. Now we had no idea what was going on, or what the next move would be. The long exhausting ride, the anticipation of seeing Peter and then the awful disappointments followed by this latest confrontation with the soldiers had made my emotions fly up and down like a yo-yo. I didn't know whether to laugh or cry. Again I found myself pushing the cork firmly down on my emotions. So, not reacting at all outwardly, I found myself saying a silent prayer for Peter, asking God to keep him alive, and asking that I might be able to see him again soon.

Without me realising it, prayer had become an integral part of my life. Whenever I was fearful or overwhelmed by events, which seemed to be happening with increasing frequency, I prayed to God. I remembered back to the time in Germany when, because there was nobody else willing to do it, I had been persuaded to help out with one of the Sunday School classes, rather than see it close. Never having gone to Sunday School as a child, I was fascinated by the facts and information supplied in order for me to prepare for the classes each week, together with the simple stories of the Bible which made a deep impression on me. Time and again the message that I learnt, and tried to put across to the children, was *God loves you and cares for you.* I knew that I needed to keep reminding myself of that truth, as I dealt with this situation. My memories of the past seemed to give me new heart.

After the soldiers had gone, we all stood around for a while discussing what to do next, knowing full well that we were really in the hands of the Iraqis. None of us liked the idea of our group being split, with some made to stay and others told to go, but we knew that we would have to deal with each new situation as seemed best for us all, and be prepared to take one step at a time.

Soon it was time to eat again! Mealtimes seemed to be one of the few fixed events to look forward to. Before the invasion had occurred I had had a fetish for food, especially chocolate. Now food was not one of my main preoccupations, and I was losing quite a bit of weight. 'Quite a good diet,' I thought to myself ruefully, 'but not one I could really recommend.'

After supper I was sitting outside my bedroom door talking to Jean when we once more became aware of the soldiers who had read out our names from the bits of paper. This brought us both hastily to our feet, eager to know what they now had to say. Women appeared like magic, and suddenly we found ourselves in a bit of a squash, listening to the soldiers' latest pronouncements.

'You will not be going anywhere tonight, but maybe tomorrow,' the taller of the two men was saying. This immediately started a round of questions from some of the women, all of which were ignored by both soldiers. I think they had had enough the previous time they had tried to tell us something. He continued as though no one had interrupted him. 'Those women whose names were called out earlier, be prepared to move tomorrow.' Without waiting for any reaction and certainly wanting to avoid having to try and answer more questions, they both turned on their heels and quickly departed to the safety of the lift!

Mike made a beeline for me, obviously with a question on his lips. 'Sheila, would you be able to organise this convoy? You know, making sure that everyone on that list has a car to travel in?'

'Yes, no problem,' I heard myself saying, grateful in a way that I had something positive to do. As Michael turned to walk away, I touched him on the arm and said, 'Mike, do you think that the men are OK?'

'Yes, I'm sure they're fine,' he said, with a smile on his face, looking me straight in the eye. I trusted Michael's judgment, which lined up with my own feelings. Returning his smile, I hurried off to organise the transport as he had requested, and to get some much-needed sleep.

I was fast asleep when a loud rap on my bedroom door woke me with a start. Fumbling for the bedside light in the pitch black, I knocked my watch off the table and sent it flying across the bedroom floor. When I found the light switch and retrieved my watch I saw it was still only five o'clock in the morning. I opened the bedroom door a fraction to see who had woken me from such a deep sleep. Staring back at me was the face of an Iraqi soldier, looking as tired as I felt. He spoke firmly in English. 'You must get up, have breakfast and go see your husband.'

'OK,' I nodded mechanically in reply. I watched as he knocked on Jean's door before I carefully closed my own door again. Andrew and Laura had slept through all of this, but I knew that we would now have to get a move on, in spite of the early hour. I suddenly felt wide awake, as the adrenaline started to pump through my body, leaving no place for sluggishness.

'Come on, lazy bones, it's time for breakfast,' I said in a sing-song voice, as I gently shook them both to get them to wake up. 'We have another short journey to make today, and we need an early start,' I explained. The last thing I wanted to do was to raise their expectations of seeing their dad, only to have them crushed again so cruelly, so I avoided mentioning Peter and the hopes that I had. But my children weren't put off that easily.

'Mum, are we going to see Daddy?' they asked hopefully.

'Maybe,' I replied cautiously as I threw their clothes on the bed.

After a frantic five minutes we were ready to vacate the room, with our bags in our hands. Quickly and quietly we made our way down to the dining room, where we met up with the other women and children who would be in our little convoy. What a motley crew we were, all from different social backgrounds, with not much in common apart from the occupations of our husbands.

Karen was at the table nearest the door with her son Paul, who seemed more interested in chatting to one of his friends than eating any breakfast. Jean was already there, too, and gave a sleepy wave to me as she tried to keep her two children interested in the food before them. Gily strolled up to Jean and exchanged a few words, while Ann, whose children were grown up and living in England, bent down and helped one of the little ones whose shoe lace had become untied. At another table sat Gina, a swimming instructor, looking wonderfully fit and alert in spite of the early hour. I remembered that it had only been a week or two since she had passed Laura for her Brownie swimming badge, and now we all shared a different kind of test together. Gina was in deep conversation with Angie, a quiet woman who I had spoken to only rarely, as our paths never seemed to cross. I knew little about her, apart from the fact that she had two teenage children. Sitting with them listening intently were Heidi and her nine-year-old daughter, who was looking quite serious as she tucked into her cereal. On another table was Sue with her two young girls and her teenage son, sharing a table with Sharon, who always seemed to have a smile on her face. She had a son and daughter, like me, and seemed to be coping well enough. As in all groups, I knew that some of the women had had their differences of opinion with each other in the past, and I hoped that whatever had previously caused division would not be a problem in the future.

We still had no idea where we were being taken, and my thoughts strayed to the women we would be leaving behind. How would they feel when they got up and found that we had left? My heart went out to them, but on the other hand I wondered what was in store for us. We had tried to prepare as much as we could. Most of us had managed to obtain some water to take with us in the cars, which would keep us going for a good few hours, although we still didn't know how long our journey would be.

The signal was given for us to leave, and with a bag over my shoulder and Andrew and Laura holding my hands, I walked out of the Al-Mansour Melia Hotel, along with the other women and children whose names had been on the list. I glanced back at the building for the last time, trying to spot any movement from the bedroom windows of the women we were leaving behind, but without success. We were all soon in the car again, and my attention turned to driving as we slowly moved away from the hotel parking lot to take yet another journey into the unknown. 'This is becoming a habit,' I thought to myself grimly, 'but one I could well do without!'

10

United at Last

Within minutes of leaving the hotel we were swallowed up in the bustling traffic of Baghdad. I was surprised how busy the city roads were, even at this early hour of the day. It took a great deal of concentration on my part to remain in the convoy and not get separated by the impatient drivers who were in a hurry to get to their destinations. I was grateful that the children quickly settled down in the back of the car, which allowed Jean and me to concentrate fully on traffic conditions. We both appreciated the friendship which had been strengthened by our bizarre circumstances. It was also fortunate that our children seemed to get on well together, I thought, as I glanced in the rear mirror and saw them lolling on each other, fast asleep.

On reaching the northern outskirts of Baghdad, the leading Iraqi car pulled into a petrol station and we all duly followed. A scurry of activity commenced as we refuelled our cars. A rumour that had been going round that our husbands were in another part of Baghdad was finally quashed by the soldiers, which didn't surprise any of us. We were now highly suspicious of anything that the Iraqis told us.

After all the cars had had their tanks filled we took the road out of Baghdad, which was the main route towards

Mosul. This we knew for sure, as Jean still had her road map, which she discreetly referred to from time to time as we went along. The wide road and lack of traffic made the going easy, until the car belonging to Sue stopped – and refused to start again. No one was particularly surprised that it had given up the ghost. In fact Sue was all for leaving it on the side of the road and travelling in the mini-bus, but our guards wouldn't hear of it.

Sue was a down-to-earth, practical lady who spoke bluntly. With an understandable edge of sarcasm in her voice, she made the point that as the Iraqis had taken virtually everything of hers anyway, to lose the car was no big deal. But the soldiers refused to believe what she told them concerning the pillaging of our homes, and were genuinely distressed at the thought of Sue losing her vehicle. So a bemused truck driver was flagged down, a piece of string, similar to that used to tie bales of hay together, was produced, carefully fastened to Sue's car and the very old farm truck, and off we went again . . . very slowly! In spite, or maybe because, of all the tension that we had experienced we couldn't help laughing at this incredible sight, and at the curious stares from other motorists on the road. After several miles even our military escorts realised the futility of this plan, and left Sue's car with the truck driver, promising her that it would be returned to her at a later date.

Our journey took us through Iraq's countryside, which was surprisingly poverty-stricken, considering the country had received so much wealth from oil, but then, I reasoned, much of the country's reserves had been spent on the war with Iran. The only real diversion from this bleak picture was Tikrit, Saddam's home town. There we saw modern, well constructed buildings in this area which looked and felt so prosperous. There were also giant-size posters of Saddam, their local hero, around every corner, his image seeming to sneer at us with contempt. Soon we had left his birthplace behind, passing massive army camps containing thousands of tanks and troops, which I realised later were there to protect Iraq's borders from any attack that Turkey might launch!

We had now been on the road for five hours, and were just wondering how much longer our journey would take when we came to an oil terminal set back from the main road. Our small convoy stopped at the gates, our guards conversing with the soldiers before we were escorted. The children started to wake up in the back of the car as we went through the gates. Surely this couldn't be our destination – an oil refinery in northern Iraq? I shuddered as I observed the great frameworks of metal and the container tanks that broke the skyline. Why an oil refinery? Filled with apprehension, we followed as we were bidden. Jean and I exchanged worried glances. Had we been unwise to leave the hotel to embark on this journey? Not even the British Embassy knew of our whereabouts. In our keenness to be with our husbands once more, had we acted too rashly?

Our new surroundings looked pretty bleak. The buildings were grey and depressing, matching my mood exactly. We got our belongings out of the car, and were told to follow an Iraqi civilian wearing a lightweight brown suit, who had an air about him of someone who seemed to be in charge. He led us through some open doors to what looked like a canteen. There we were told by an Iraqi soldier, in a friendly tone, to sit down, and he would bring us some food and water. In spite of his kind approach and the food that eventually arrived, none of us now believed anything that the Iraqis said to us, and we all declared that we had no intention of eating anything until we knew what was going on.

A general chorus of 'Where are our husbands?' went up as we scowled our displeasure at our new Iraqi guards. One of the soldiers, obviously not used to having women act in this way, said nervously, 'They are having lunch.'

'We don't believe you,' said Gily, putting all our thoughts into words.

The guards looked baffled, and one of them, not much more than a teenager I guessed, asked in obvious innocence why we thought they would lie to us. We then started to regale them with some of the things that we had had to endure in rather less than patient voices. They of course had no idea what we had been through prior to arriving here, and our young guard looked confused, saying with all apparent sincerity that he would never lie to us. Suddenly, at the height of this exchange, the doors at the end of the room opened with a bang as they hit the wall, allowing an impatient mass of bodies to burst through. All eyes turned towards the sound.

There, standing in the doorway and now moving towards us at great speed, were a crowd of men, some with huge grins on their faces, others with a frown as they scanned our group to see who they could spot. At last we were being united with our husbands! The next few moments were lost in highly charged emotion, together with tears, laughter, hugs and kisses, as husbands and wives, children and dads were reunited once again, in the most unlikely of settings. I ran into Peter's arms with tears streaming down my face. He pulled me to him and for a moment we were lost in our emotions, blocking out the rest of the world. Andrew and Laura were hugging Peter's waist, shouting 'Daddy, Daddy!' All around us, similar scenes were being played out as families united once more. Tears flowed freely, and even the guards were overwhelmed by the depth of the emotions they were witnessing. Embarrassed by the tears that started to flow down their own faces, they tactfully left the room for a while.

After a few moments when we told each other how much we loved and had missed each other, and Peter had given both of our kids big hugs, we started to relate a little more calmly. It was so good to see Peter again, to hear his voice with his unmistakable Middlesbrough accent, and to watch the laugh-lines form when he smiled. He looked fit and relaxed, and not at all stressed by the events that he had gone through since we last met. Nevertheless, he expressed his concern at our forced separation.

'I've been that worried about you all,' he said. 'I kept wondering how long it would be before we met again. When I saw our car sitting outside this building I couldn't believe my eyes. How did you get here?'

I grinned, and made a gesture of helplessness with my hands indicating that I had no idea where to begin. We had so much news to catch up on. But as thrilled as I was to see Peter, I was equally aware that all around us stood twenty men who were bitterly disappointed that their wives were not with us. I pulled away reluctantly from him for a few moments, to give what positive information I could about their wives. Jackie's husband Gerry stood nearby, looking understandably concerned. I was able to quickly tell him that Jackie was fine, and was waiting for him in the hotel in Baghdad. I managed to speak to several of the other men before the guards, who had now returned, shepherded them outside. They were told to get back on the bus that had just brought them from where they had been staying, so that they could be taken to Baghdad and reunited with *their* families. We wished them well as they departed. I hoped with all my heart that they would all be together again very soon, as the Iraqis had promised, and said a silent prayer for them on their journey.

Once their bus had departed we all trooped back into the canteen. The guards explained that our accommodation was not yet ready, as it was being cleaned. Unperturbed, we sat round a small table, trying to catch up on all the happenings of the last two weeks. We found ourselves all trying to talk at the same time, with none of it making much sense! It was just good to be together again, and to know that the events of the last two weeks were finally behind us. I was more than glad to hand responsibility for the family back to Peter, knowing that he would be able to deal with whatever cropped up from now on in his own dependable, relaxed way.

After Peter had spent time with Laura and Andrew, finding out how they were and what they had been doing, they got a little bored sitting around listening to us nattering on, and drifted off to play with some of their friends whose parents were also trying to catch up on events. Pleased that they were relaxed enough not to want to cling to Peter, I sat back and listened as he shared a little of what had been happening to him since we last met.

He told me that after he had left us that night – to go to a meeting, so he thought – he was immediately confronted by a couple of soldiers with rifles who escorted him to the middle of the camp, where other men had already gathered, together with a small group of teenagers. Soon more of his colleagues were added to the group, with the Iraqi soldiers getting quite agitated, shouting abuse and beginning to throw their weight around.

'There were some lads who were only just teenagers in the group, Sheila,' said Peter, with a certain amount of feeling in his voice. 'You'll know some of them by sight, I expect. They're more adolescents than men, and we pleaded with the soldiers to let them go back to their homes, which they eventually agreed to. I felt much better once that one had been sorted.'

Then Peter confirmed that they had been taken to

what had been the police station but was now the Iraqi headquarters. When they arrived they saw men sitting on the side of the road with their hands and feet tied up. He said that a few had obviously been beaten, some quite badly. I found myself suddenly shivering as Peter let that fact be known, and, in order to compose myself again, got him to break off for a moment while I checked what the children were doing. I wanted to hear everything that he had to say, but didn't want him to feel that I was reacting badly in any way.

'We were taken inside and questioned quite roughly, but we weren't beaten or anything like that,' he said, giving me a reassuring grin, as he continued his story. 'We tried to tell them who we were, explaining that we weren't active soldiers but that we were advisors, which after a while the Iraqis seemed to accept. We thought at this point we were over the worst, until Mike came to tell us that we were not going to be allowed to go back to the camp. I half thought that he was joking at first, but I could tell from the look in his eyes that he wasn't. He'd been told that they were going to take us to Baghdad, and we all said "absolutely no way" – in slightly stronger language than that! – but we realised in the end that it was no use. We were their prisoners, and would have to do what we were ordered to do.'

Peter started to laugh, and I couldn't imagine what he could have found to be so funny about being taken to Baghdad as a hostage. Seeing my look of puzzlement, he stopped laughing and explained.

'Well, you see, we were all put on this bus, which was the first stage of our journey to Iraq. The route took us past the fish market, which as you know is just before the turning to go to the camp. As we got to the camp, all the men shouted to the bus driver, "Turn, turn," and he started to steer the bus into the road leading back to camp! The Iraqi soldiers' immediate reaction was to turn round and point their rifles at us because of the instructions we had been shouting to the driver, so we all ducked for cover and then started shouting, "Stop, stop," and the bus stopped and continued on its original route. It was then we realised that there was just no way that we were going to get back to you for some time. We also found out that the Iraqi soldiers had no sense of humour!'

I could just imagine Peter and the rest of his mates doing things like that, partly to see what would happen, and partly to show that they just weren't cowed by their captors. I didn't even want to begin to imagine what might have happened if the bus had jerked suddenly while guns were pointed at the men, or if anyone had made a move which had been seen as threatening to the Iraqis. Some things are best not even thought about. My thoughts were interrupted by Peter's continuation of his story.

'There were so many men on that bus, Sheila, worse than Middlesbrough in the rush hour,' he quipped. 'And that driver! I don't know where he passed his test, but I have a sneaking suspicion that it was on the back of a camel! I think someone must have given him orders to head for every pothole he could see. It was a bit like being on the fairground at Blackpool at times. Every corner we came to, we went round on two wheels. All that was missing was the candy floss.'

Peter was laughing again, and my hunch that he would have made the best of whatever situation he was in was being confirmed in the news he was starting to share with me. I listened with interest as he finished his tale. He told me that they were eventually put on a plane to Baghdad before getting another bus which took them to the hotel where we had expected to find them. They had all been treated reasonably well, and had been allowed to use the swimming pool each day. Peter had got into the habit of jogging as part of his daily fitness routine, and he was allowed to run round the inside perimeter of the hotel, usually with Michael. This allowed them both not only to get some proper exercise but to get rid of some of the tension and emotion that all the men were feeling having been taken so suddenly and forcefully from their loved ones, with not even a chance of saying a proper goodbye.

I began to tell him all the things that we had been up to. It was now his turn to look shocked or amazed or distressed, depending on which bit I was relaying.

Time passed quickly as we caught up with all our news and just enjoyed each other's company. I glanced round occasionally and saw the other families deep in conversation. The troubled, weary frowns were being replaced by smiles as they once again spent time with those they loved. I could feel some of the tension slipping away from me as I appreciated afresh Peter's presence, and the fact that we were united once again as a family. Every so often laughter punctuated the air, as events were related that had caused someone to see the funny side of things for a while. We were all so engrossed in our catching up that it hardly seemed possible, when I looked at my watch, to realise that almost five hours had elapsed since we first sat down to talk. Someone must be doing a good job of getting our accommodation ready, I thought, wondering, with a smile, whether they were having a massive clear-up, like teenagers after they have been left at home without Mum and Dad!

Eventually the doors opened and three Iraqi men dressed in civilian clothes walked into the centre of the room. All the chatter stopped as we strained to hear what they had to say. 'The first bus is ready to take you now,' one of the men was saying in a heavily accented voice. 'Listen for your names, then go and get on the bus. Please move quickly.'

The happy relaxed atmosphere that we had enjoyed for the last few hours evaporated within minutes, now we were again being told what to do by our captors. Our names were called, and I was pleased to hear that Jean's family were also to be travelling on our bus. We gathered up our things and walked outside to the bus, Peter giving Laura a hand to help her up the high step. Andrew bounced up the steps and promptly sat on the seat next to the door, only to be moved along when an armed guard indicated he had to sit there!

As we settled ourselves, I noticed that only about half of the families in the convoy I had come with were on the bus. I thought it was strange that they hadn't yet boarded, and was just about to make a remark about it to Peter when the guard who had been so baffled when we said that we had been lied to, got on the bus. There were tears in his eyes as he spoke. 'I am so sorry,' was all that he managed to say, before he gulped and rushed away. I looked at Peter with concern, my heart doing its usual nosedive into my boots! What was going on now?

The bus struggled into life and we began to move forward. But not, as we had been told, to another part of the camp, but out again through the main gates. So that was it. No wonder the guards were upset. They too had come to the realisation that they could be lied to and deceived. As individuals, they had promised us that we would be safe on their camp, and now they obviously felt that they had betrayed our trust. I felt that these men had been genuine, decent people; like us, they had no way of knowing what lay in store for them in the future.

By now I was starting to expect the unexpected, and although I was far from happy with this new turn of events

I was far too weary to dwell on it for long. Peter went and sat with Andrew near the front of the bus, Laura sat with her friend Helen, and I sat on my own not far away. Just behind me were Jean and her husband Sean, and as I turned round to speak to them I realised that they were once again studying the map to see if they could work out where we were being taken. I turned back again, knowing that they would let me know if they came up with any definite information. At one point we drove through a valley flanked on either side of the road by rugged mountainous terrain. Dotted along this area were many machine-guns on tripods. It flashed through my mind that maybe we were going to be shot at some point – how I wished that I had a mind that was less imaginative. Why had I watched so many adventure films on television? This area looked like the place where the bandits always holed up.

After several hours of travelling, just as it was getting dark, the bus tried to pull into another oil refinery, but we were obviously not expected and after much heated discussion and arm-waving at the gates we set off again, this time back down the way we had come. After another half-hour had passed, the bus drove down a small lane and eventually through some large gates held open by armed soldiers. We came to a stop. It was pitch black by now, so seeing where we were was difficult, but I could just about make out the shape of some buildings. One of the armed soldiers who had been our escort opened the door of the bus and disappeared into the darkness. Soon he was back, holding a piece of paper from which he read aloud the names of all those families present.

Sean and Jean and their children were first, and as their names were read out they followed a guard into the darkness. My heart went out to my good friend and her family when I saw the tiredness and uncertainty that was etched into their features, as they made an effort to keep up with the guard while at the same time guiding their now sleepy children in the right direction. One by one all our names were called, and soon it was our turn to follow a guard to the place where we would be spending the night.

The soldier opened the door, stepped into the house and flicked an electric switch. Immediately light flooded the dirty, dull interior. I was to find out later that these houses had been constructed some years before to house Russian workers. I can't think that they shed many tears when it was time for them to go. I mustn't get pessimistic, I thought to myself as I looked around the room. I didn't want to spoil our first night together for some time by feeling depressed. Anyway, on second glance, things weren't so bad. In the main room was a metal bed frame with a brand-new mattress, still in its plastic wrap, along with pillows and a couple of sheets. We'd manage.

We found that this new 'home' of ours had two further bedrooms both containing single beds. There was a small bathroom which looked as though it could do with a good scrub, and the room next to that was the toilet. It was in a pretty disgusting state, but at least it was a flush toilet, rather than just a hole in the ground, which is quite common in that part of the world.

Before departing, the soldier had asked if we wanted anything to eat. Did we ever! I and the children hadn't eaten anything save for a few biscuits since breakfast, and our throats were parched. We asked for some food and some bottled water. The soldier said that he would see what he could do, and quickly departed into the night.

Peter made the children laugh, chasing them round the rest of the house as they explored every room and cupboard. As I watched him playing with them, it was obvious that his Christian faith was as strong as ever, and he had not wavered in his belief that all would eventually turn out well for us. I knew that, try as I might, I felt differently to him. I hoped, of course, that things would ultimately be OK, but I wasn't convinced of that fact and I envied Peter his cool, calm confidence and faith, which I knew so little about.

But questions of faith and future would have to wait, as I felt there were more important things to attend to. I had noticed immediately on entering the house that the windows lacked any curtains, giving us absolutely no privacy. But I still had my tartan car rug, so we managed to roughly cover the main window, which made the place feel a little less like a goldfish bowl. I felt desperately tired, and it was all that I could do to get Andrew and Laura ready for bed. I said a quick prayer of thanks that we were all together again, before tucking them up and kissing them goodnight.

The promised food and water had not materialised, but by now anything that was promised I took with a pinch of salt. I was just too tired even to clean my teeth, and climbed into bed fully clothed! I'm not sure what Peter felt about this, but the only thought on my mind was sleep and plenty of it. I hoped that a good long rest would begin to dispel some of the tension that I had been feeling of late.

I must have been deeply asleep about an hour later when the door to the house nearly flew off its hinges from the banging made by the soldier returning with our long-awaited food. I shot bolt upright with a scream, all my worst fears being confirmed in the noise that he made. He handed the tray to a half-awake Peter and was gone in a moment. On it were some chicken, bread and bottled water. After we had taken a little of each, we settled back down to sleep. Within a few moments all I could hear was Peter's even breathing and the sound of crickets outside in the cool night air. I lay reflecting what the future days might hold for us all.

We had all lived through such dramatic days already. How was it all going to end, I wondered as I drifted off to sleep. There was no way of knowing then, of course, that we had already become part of Saddam Hussein's 'human shield', and the effects that that would have on me in particular in the future. I didn't know where we were, or for what purpose. Least of all did I know how long it would be before we saw Britain again. All I knew right now was that I had my family around me again, and that I was very, very tired.

11

Saddam's Human Shield

For a moment I couldn't think where I was when I woke the following morning. My sleep had been fitful and disturbed. Then I felt Peter's back pressed against mine and I remembered all that had happened the night before as I gave the blanket a tug, thinking that it had been quite a while since I had to fight for my share of the bedclothes. The sun, which had been up for hours, was etching patterns on the walls as it crept in through the sides of our makeshift curtains. This was the start of a brand-new day, and I was happy that we were all alive to see it. As I reflected on things that had passed, I realised that most of what I had worried about had not actually happened. Here I was in northern Iraq with Peter and our children in some old shack in the middle of nowhere. We were hostages, but we were safe for the time being at least.

My attention was caught by the sound of vehicles moving outside, and what sounded like digging! Pulling myself out of bed, I sleepily made my way over to the window. Peering round the end of the tartan blanket, I was amazed at what I saw. The area outside our house was alive with activity. Some Iraqi labourers were hard at work digging trenches around the inside perimeter of our gardens, causing small rivulets of sweat to drip from their faces. Others were painting the iron fence black. And to my even greater amazement lorries were tipping piles of rubble down on what had been a mud road. Before my eyes it was being laid into a solid surface and, as I watched, a road roller could be seen coming through the gates.

I shouted to Peter to come and see what was happening. He jumped out of bed and joined me at the window, pulling more of the blanket back so he could see in greater detail what was going on. Taking it all in for a moment, he said, as he slipped his arm around my waist, 'Well, I guess this is home for a while.' I sighed inwardly, sensing that he was right.

We were now joined by Andrew and Laura, who had also been woken by the activity that suddenly surrounded us all. After a few more moments watching everything that was going on, I left the three of them still looking out of the window, and went to get a wash. Soon we were all ready to have breakfast, and we opened the door, stepping gingerly outside for the first time in the daylight. The men stopped their work, pausing for a moment from their tasks as they eyed us up and down before returning to their toils. An Iraqi soldier in his early thirties walked towards us, half-smiling as he gestured for us to follow him. We did as he indicated, Peter grabbing hold of my hand as Andrew and Laura jumped a hole that had not yet been filled in the road.

We entered a chalet that was now acting as a dining room. Places were set out along a long table, with yet more places set in a small alcove. Jean and her family soon joined us, and within a short time all five families that now shared this camp were ready and waiting for their food. The meal was simple that first morning with fruit, in the form of water melons, and bread, but as other meals came along they became more interesting. Instead of potatoes, we had rice, and lots of it, every day, and a very strange-looking meat which I had never come across in any of the different countries I had lived in previously. I didn't have the courage to enquire about its identity in case my knowledge would have made it impossible for me to eat it!

As well as the melons, which we had in abundance, there were figs, some of which were made into fig jam, making an interesting change each morning from Golden Shred marmalade! There was also beer to drink. I am not a beer drinker, finding the taste fairly unpleasant, but I discovered that it made a welcome alternative to the bottled water that we were given, apart from the very welcome cup of tea that was usually served after meals.

I'm not sure what occupation the men who prepared our meals had before we arrived, but I'm pretty certain that they weren't chefs! Not only did they cook the food, but they acted as waiters during the meal, serving each course that they had prepared in the kitchen. We nicknamed one of our 'waiters' Manuel, after the character from the BBC comedy *Fawlty Towers*; he sloshed the food around and generally managed to get into a complete muddle most mealtimes, poor chap. The propaganda going round was that the Allied troops were starving the women and children of Iraq, and I felt bad when the men who had served us ate what we had left from the containers that they had been serving from. Seeing what was happening, we made sure that there was always plenty of food left for them.

We found that we were indeed near an oil refinery, although thankfully it was out of sight of where we were being held. There was another small cluster of buildings near ours, which did not have armed guards on the gates as ours did. We guessed that this other camp housed the workers at the oil refinery. The scenery that surrounded us was uninspiring scrubland, with a few radio antennae dotted here and there.

Over the next few days we came to expect the bizarre from our guards. After a good road surface was laid, they erected streetlights in record time. They provided us with a volleyball net and a table-tennis table. They even planted flowers in the 45°C heat, none of which had a chance of survival. Our men started to play volleyball every morning, joined by one of the guards – and me! I knew that I needed exercise, and this seemed to be a good way of getting it, although what the guards thought about a lone Western woman playing with a group of men each day I dread to think.

One of the buildings was made into a laundry room complete with an old twin-tub washing machine, which became a daily meeting and contact point for the wives as we did our washing, and yet another former dwelling was made into a medical room where a lady doctor visited most mornings for half a hour. They even put an old TV into the room where we ate our food. The Iraqi guards used to switch this on while we were having our meals; we tried to find out what was going on in the outside world, but every news programme just seemed to be full of propaganda about how the Iraqis were winning the war, and how awful the Allied troops were. Free speech was not allowed in Iraq, and yet one evening we saw a demonstration taking place in London, where Iraqis were carrying placards condemning the action of the Allied troops. We knew that it would be totally out of the question for any of us to try and do a similar thing anywhere in Iraq.

One day when we were eating our food, pictures came on to the TV screen which got the guards excited, and they started to make gestures to indicate that we should look at the set. And there, in great clarity, we saw some friends of ours, including little Stuart Lockwood, the young son of one couple that we knew well. The family had come up with us from Kuwait. Stuart's father was in the RAF and they were now staying somewhere in Baghdad. The images that we were seeing were flashed all around the world, with Saddam stroking Stuart's hair, and asking him if he was getting his milk ration. The Western news media claimed that Stuart was looking pale and ill at ease because of the attention that Saddam was giving him, but we knew Stuart to be fairly shy anyway, so the pictures that we saw didn't cause us any great discomfort. We were just pleased to see our friends again, and to know that the women and children had been united with their menfolk. From then on, we too would watch the TV to try and catch some of these broadcasts.

One that we saw a little while later was of a wedding. A British couple had decided to get married, and the Iraqi news service covered the wedding reception. Dougie, Pat's husband, was the best man, and the pastor of the church we had attended before the conflict officiated. I squealed with delight when I saw Pat, looking very happy and eating chips! 'Some people have all the luck,' I said, laughing. 'When was the last time we got to eat any chips?'

'Give us a chip, Pat,' shouted Peter at the TV, and we all laughed again. By this time I'm sure the guards thought we had gone completely mad, but we were just so thrilled to see our friends again, alive and well.

The guards holding us were clearly determined to make life as pleasant for us as they could. This was confirmed when one of the young soldiers, in halting English, announced that Saddam had instructed them to make us feel as at home as possible, and therefore he wanted us to make a list of anything that we lacked. We stared at him for a moment in disbelief, wondering if this was some kind of joke, but no, he was deadly serious. Pen and paper were produced, and we were asked to write down anything that we needed and they would do their best to help us.

Soon our pens were red hot as we wrote down things that we could do with – socks, underwear for the children, curtains for the windows, toothbrushes and the like. All was duly noted, and within a short time nearly everything that we had asked for had been received. It was then that Peter started to get really bold – or maybe I should say downright cheeky! The next day when one of the guards asked if there was anything that we required Peter stepped forward and said, 'Yes, there is something that I would like. I am a Christian, and I would like to attend a Christian service. You Iraqis are Moslem, and pray to Allah five times a day, so you know the importance of prayer. Christians also need to pray, and I would like the opportunity to pray to our God in a church, preferably at an Anglican service.' All eyes turned on the guard, who was nodding his head to indicate that he understood what Peter had said. He left, saying that he would see what he could do. Within a few hours he was back, saying that everything had been arranged, and we could go tomorrow, which happened to be a Sunday, to a Christian church service in town! Now it was our turn to look surprised and delighted as we had never imagined that this request would be granted.

The next day, at the appointed time, a coach duly appeared, and our little family, together with the other families we were with, boarded the coach to go to the service. It has to be said that some on that coach would not normally be found in a church on a Sunday morning, but I think they saw it as an outing, an opportunity to get off the camp for a while. We were driven to the town of Kirkuk, several miles away from our camp. The coach made its way slowly down the backstreets of the town until it came to a small European-style Catholic church building, squeezed between more conventional Iraqi buildings. We must have looked a strange sight to the locals as we stepped off the coach; some of them stared openly at us, wondering, I suppose, who we were and what we were doing there.

When we got inside we were welcomed by the priest. He was a lovely man and went out of his way to make us feel as welcome as possible. Peter explained that we weren't Catholics, and the priest said that was not a problem, he would give us an Anglican-type service instead! Soon we were joined by five other families, who we had last seen at the oil refinery we were taken to when we first came up north. It was so good to see them again. We discovered that they were now at a camp just a few miles away from Kirkuk. There were tears of joy and hugs as we greeted Gily and Karen and their families, making a firm resolution to try and meet up at their camp, especially when we discovered that *they* had a swimming pool!

The service was wonderful. The priest really was a true man of God, leading the prayers in English, one of the many languages that he knew, with real sincerity. Peter read the lesson, and we all felt uplifted and strengthened by the time the service was over.

Family anniversaries come and go, whether one is living on a housing estate in London or as a hostage in northern Iraq. Helen, Jean and Sean's daughter, had her eighth birthday a few days after the church service. The guards were told about her special day, and a birthday cake was duly produced, along with some toys for her to play with. She had a little party, and seemed to enjoy herself in spite of the odd surroundings.

A few days after that was our twelfth wedding anniversary. To our surprise and delight everyone made cards from coloured pencils and paper that they had scrounged, and they gave us little bunches of flowers and other small gifts, showing in any way possible how much they cared. Their kindness touched us both. I reminded Peter that when we had got married he had predicted that we would probably go to a lot of different places during our life together, but neither of us could ever have guessed where we would be celebrating our twelfth anniversary!

The children soon adjusted to having Peter around again, and seemed to accept the strange environment that we were in. There was, however, one pressing problem on Laura's mind. She tackled me about it one evening as she got ready for bed. 'Mum, I really would like to be home for my birthday, and to spend the day with Nana and Granddad,' she said earnestly. 'I remembered that you said that we should pray for the things that we want, so I've prayed for that!'

I stared at her, not knowing what to say. I knew that Laura thought a lot of my parents and would love to spend her special day with them, as she had in other years. But Laura's birthday was only a week away, on 3 September to be precise, and I was already thinking what I would say to the children when we couldn't give them a *Christmas* present this year. Now I had a dilemma. If I told her that she shouldn't pray that kind of prayer, I would be weakening her faith, and yet if I agreed and it didn't happen . . . So I smiled, and mumbled something about us never knowing what God might do, and hoped that when the day came she would be able to cope.

Andrew continued his knack of getting into difficult situations with supreme ease. One day, he came into the house after he had been playing with his friends for a while, with a black scorpion in a jam jar. Quite proud of what he had caught, he showed it to Peter, who looked up from what he was doing, glanced at it and said, 'Um, quite nice,' before returning to his writing. Hoping for a slightly more enthusiastic response, he then showed it to me. I thought it was anything but nice, and told him in no uncertain terms to take it outside – at once! Fed up that no one seemed interested, he thought as a last resort he would show it to some of the soldiers working nearby. He certainly got a reaction from them. They almost went crazy! Apparently the creature that Andrew was casually carrying around with him had the capability to kill an adult with its poison within twenty minutes if the victim was not attended to – and we were many miles from the nearest hospital. One of the guards grabbed the jam jar from Andrew, turning quite white as he did so, and took the scorpion off to be destroyed. Our son certainly knew how to make his mark wherever he went!

After a while life seemed to settle into some sort of routine. There would be a game of volleyball in the morning, followed by lunch, after which I would gather up the washing, take it to the laundry room and have a chat with the other wives. In spite of the occasional excitement from Andrew, life started to get a little mundane. So, to liven things up a little, Peter and I decided to organise a social evening for the adults.

We had been given a few packs of playing cards by our ever-helpful guards, and so decided to have an evening of whist. We managed to beg a few packets of crisps and some biscuits which we put in bowls, to make it look as welcoming as we could. The evening seemed to be going well, when suddenly, about halfway through, some guards rushed through the door, telling us to turn the television on immediately!

There on the screen were Jackie and Gerry and their children Rachel and Colin, together with some other friends we had been separated from. Our game of whist was quickly forgotten as we got as close to the set as we could in order to see and hear what was going on. Saddam was speaking first to Jackie and then to Rachel, who was five that day, and asking them if they had everything they wanted and whether everything was all right. Then the questions were asked more generally, and some of the women said that although they had everything they needed in terms of clothes and food, what they all wanted most of all was their freedom.

As the cameras zoomed in on Saddam, he suddenly declared that all the women and children currently being held in Iraq could return to their home country. And, because it was Rachel's birthday, he said her dad, Gerry, could go back with them, although the rest of the men must remain.

Although the Iraqi guards were now almost dancing around the room, saying that we could go back to England, we had not fully understood what Saddam had meant, and in any case we were sceptical about any promises that were made, especially as it seemed such a spur-of-the-moment comment on a 'live' TV broadcast. So we were very matter-of-fact about the whole thing, and didn't allow ourselves to get excited about this latest twist in our circumstances, much to the puzzlement of our guards.

The next day the soldiers were just as excited as they had been the night before. It was almost as though they were being released, rather than us. We really knew that something was happening, though, when one of the guards came to Peter and the other men and asked them to write down the names of their wives and children. This was done, and the guard went away again, only to come back a few hours later to say that all the women and children would be leaving in half an hour's time! So we had just thirty minutes to adjust to the news, pack, and say goodbye to our husbands, who would be forced to remain.

I had very mixed feelings about the whole thing. On the one hand I wanted to go home, especially to get my children out of this dangerous situation, in spite of the fact that they seemed to be handling it extremely well. I wanted to see my parents and to be able to do what I wanted, when I wanted, without having to think about the restrictions that the Iraqis put on us. On the other hand, I didn't want to leave Peter. I realised more than ever what a help and a strength he was to me, and I couldn't bear the thought of being parted from him again.

But my practical husband, cool and businesslike to the end, wouldn't hear about my desire to stay with him in Iraq. Instead he sat down with me, and talked me through all the practicalities of returning to the UK without him. He told me what money I could expect to come in each month, how to pay the bills, what letters to give to the bank regarding our joint account, and so on.

All too soon the time passed, and the coach that would take us back to Baghdad arrived slightly earlier than they had said, making the whole time a little shorter. My discomfort at leaving Peter behind was not helped by the fact that Sue had decided to stay on with her husband, causing me to feel torn about my decision to return to England all over again.

What a forlorn group we were as we boarded the coach. All the wives and children were shedding inconsolable tears, while the men looked anxious but tried to put on a brave face. Even some of guards looked upset at the hard decision that we were all having to make.

The coach moved off and I gave a final wave to Peter, hugging the children closer to me, not knowing how long it would be before we saw each other again. We were taken back to the Al-Mansour Melia Hotel, where we checked into our old room and waited for the first flight back to

Britain. From time to time, other groups of women would arrive from where they had been detained throughout the country. Some had been taken to the camp where we knocked two houses into one, and we were told that some of the houses had had to be demolished after our departure. Some women had been taken to the camp with only the clothes that they stood up in, and therefore made use of anything that they found. Jean was staggered when she walked into the dining room one lunchtime to see a lady sitting there, waiting for lunch, wearing Jean's clothes! Although Jean understood the situation she naturally found it a bit of a shock at first.

We eventually linked up with all the women that we had been with before the invasion of Kuwait started. I was dying to quiz Pat about the wedding she had attended with her family, and about those delicious-looking chips!

'You lucky thing,' I teased, 'we were never given chips where we were. I doubt whether Manuel knew what they were.' After I had explained to a puzzled Pat who Manuel was, she told us the true story of that wedding reception.

'We hadn't eaten at all that day before the chips arrived,' said Pat, laughing, 'and when they came, there were so few, and by this time we were so hungry. I would have died for some of Manuel's rice, even if half of it would have ended up on my lap.' We all laughed, realising that things aren't always what the TV camera seems to portray.

Finally the word came that a flight was ready for us, and a few days after we had arrived at the hotel we boarded an Iraqi Airlines Boeing 747 going to London, Paris and Washington. We were on our way home, with very mixed feelings.

We weren't the only foreign nationals being allowed to go home. Saddam had offered the same deal to the American women whose husbands were based in Kuwait, and the black American senator, Jesse Jackson, was on our flight, escorting the American women home and no doubt picking up a few votes along the way. The media, in the form of newspapermen and TV cameramen, were in full force as we left the hotel, and again when we were at the airport waiting to board our flight. Embassy officials had instructed us not to talk to the press or TV people, as our husbands were in the armed forces. I was too upset about leaving Peter to want to give any interviews, anyway.

Gerry was, as far as I knew, the only Englishman on that flight. Poor man, he was of course happy to be with Jackie and their children, but mortified that he was the only male who had been released, feeling terribly guilty that he was free and the others weren't. But no resentment was felt towards him or his family. On the contrary, we were pleased for them, knowing that they would be able to start to rebuild their lives a little before the rest of us.

Sitting on the plane as it sped through the air, I wondered what kind of future we were all flying into. Apart from still being concerned about Peter, I wondered how much my parents knew about our whereabouts, as getting word back to them in England had been impossible. But, as I was increasingly to find out, God has many different ways of dealing with problems. Although I had deliberately turned my back on the cameras so I would have no chance of being interviewed, Laura, in mischievous excitement, had faced them and given the assembled cameramen a cheery wave, unknowingly signalling to my mum and dad back in Britain that we were safe and well and on our way back. No wonder Laura was excited. We were flying home on 2 September, the day before her birthday, so she would be with her Nana and Granddad for her special day, just as she had prayed.

12

Return of the Reluctant Heroes

As we landed on the runway at Heathrow Airport I was aware that my heart was filled with conflicting emotions. One moment I felt just so relieved to be back on English soil, and the next moment a wave of deep sadness would sweep over me as I remembered that Peter was still held hostage in Iraq. I had not been able to throw off guilty thoughts at leaving him behind, in spite of the fact that I had no real choice in the matter. It would have been totally irresponsible to stay with the children in that situation; deep down I knew I had made the right decision, but that didn't stop my heart from aching.

As the plane taxied to the point where we would all disembark, I was astounded to see dozens of reporters all clamouring to get a better viewing position of us leaving the aircraft. The slight tension I felt at having to face this onslaught was broken for a moment by the unintentional humour created by the Iraqi air hostess, intoning into the public address system on the aircraft the standard farewell greeting that she hoped we had had a pleasant flight and that we would fly again with Iraqi Airlines some time in the future! 'Not if I can help it!' I thought as I sorted my hand luggage out, keeping an eye on Andrew and Laura as we all waited for the plane to slowly empty.

A bank of cameras faced us as we got off the plane. Flashlights popped repeatedly, the strong electronic light seeming like some freak lightning storm. Cameramen shouted for us to look their way, and jostled with each other for the best picture angles. I felt completely overwhelmed and more than a little bemused. So people in England did know some of what had been happening, after all! Several airport hostesses came up to us and gave us warm words of welcome. The reception that we were getting was one usually reserved for returning heroes, but we felt more like deserters, acutely aware of those we had left behind. If the reporters expected us to wave joyfully, we must have left them feeling very disappointed. We were headline news, but would have much preferred to slip quietly back into the country, without any fuss. Reporters wanted to ask us questions, as they had before we left Iraq, but, heeding the advice of the British Embassy staff that any wrong interpretation on what we said could endanger our husbands' lives, we refrained from saying anything. Eventually one of the airport staff came to the rescue. She pushed through the scrum of reporters and asked if we were part of the BLT (British Liaison Team); when I said we were, we were all quickly shepherded on to a waiting bus. We were asked not to leave the airport before a debriefing with a member of the armed forces had been completed.

Most of the army and air force military who were previously living in Kuwait but had been out of the country during the invasion now had the job of supporting and helping the wives and children who had husbands held in Iraq. The army and air force together had organised an information line in London a couple of weeks earlier, and it was from here that they had been in contact with our families in England. This had been of great help and comfort to my parents, especially as the people who phoned them were people who knew us personally. They had told my parents that we as a family had been together in a hotel in Baghdad for the last two and a half weeks! Obviously the Foreign Office had got that one a bit wrong, but at least it helped my parents through a tough time. Now these channels of information and help would transfer to us, the returning spouses. They would be used to support us and to pass on any new information regarding our husbands. I really appreciated the constant support they gave me through a very difficult time in my life, and cannot praise them highly enough.

The bus took us away from the noise and flashing bulbs of the reporters, and when we got off we walked through a doorway to be met by shouts and cheers. But this time the greeting was coming from friends. Some were those who had been with the military working in Kuwait, but at the time of the invasion were fortunately out of the country on holiday. It was great to see them again, and we greeted each other with many hugs and kisses. I spotted Martin, the friend whose house we had been staying in when the invasion started, and whose personal possessions we had tried to save as best we could. Fond of diving, he was very fit, and I could see his dark hair and pleasant smile as he stood in the crowd. I was still carrying in my handbag a few photos of his, together with a small oil painting of his children, which I fished out of the bag and handed to him. He looked blankly at them for a few seconds, mumbled something and then hurried away. I wasn't quite sure what to make of his behaviour, but later his wife Vicki enlightened me. Martin had been quite overwhelmed that I had taken the trouble to think of their possessions in spite of all that we were going through, and was too choked up to say anything to me!

Another old friend waiting to greet me was Colonel

Stewart-Wilson. It had been over twenty years since I had worked as a nanny for the Colonel and his wife, and yet here he was, waiting to welcome me home. It was a delight to see him again. He was dressed smartly in a suit, still retaining the demeanour of one who had spent most of his life in the armed forces. Although continuing to work for the military, he now held the honoured position of equerry to the Queen. He quickly explained that he was there representing my parents, who had suffered quite a lot of stress and worry since the invasion had taken place and we had become hostages. He told me that they were well, but they just couldn't face the drive to Heathrow Airport, and all the hassle that they would have had to cope with as far as red tape and reporters were concerned. As only one person was permitted to meet each returning family, they were grateful to Colonel Stewart-Wilson for undertaking this task, and eagerly awaited our return to their home.

In spite of the one-person rule, Peter's brother Paul and his wife Denise, along with Peter's sister Julie and her husband Michael, had managed to talk their way into the arrivals lounge, having driven from the north of England in the hopes of seeing us. After we had spent a short time with them, assuring them of Peter's welfare, I made a phone call to my parents. I'm not sure that what I said to them made a lot of sense, but it was so good to hear their voices again, and to know that we would all soon be back together again.

I was then led off for a debriefing session with the army personnel people, who quizzed me on all that we had been through, as well as wanting to know things like what kind of uniforms the Iraqis were wearing and what tanks and weapons were around. Fatigue was setting in, and I started to feel like a zombie! Finally they seemed satisfied with the answers that I had given them and I was at last free to go, with another reminder from them **not** to talk to the media!

I spotted Jean, who had just been united with her brother, along with other friends who were being united with their family members. I made my way over to her, this time to say goodbye. Our extreme circumstances had forged a strong bond between us, and saying goodbye was difficult. We had shared some tough times together and had supported each other, sharing our hopes and fears, and sometimes our tears. I knew that nobody would quite be able to understand what we had gone through together. But now we would have to look to others to give us the support we would need. We hugged each other and promised to keep in touch. Saying goodbye to the others was equally painful, and I was glad that it couldn't be prolonged as the Colonel was waiting to take us in his car to Mum and Dad's house.

While I had been busy in the debriefing session with the army, Andrew and Laura had been plied with chocolates and Coke by well-meaning airport officials. I knew that Andrew suffered on occasions with travel sickness, and hoped that the next couple of hours would *not* be one of those times! Airport staff had also showered them with teddy bears and bags of toys, which they gripped tightly in their chocolate-covered hands. Before I knew what was happening I was guided through the photographers into the Colonel's car, clutching a 'Welcome Home' balloon and some flowers. The children clambered into the car, the newly presented bag of toys the only belongings they possessed in the world. TV cameras whirred as we waved goodbye to Peter's family and we set off to be united with my parents.

13

Long-distance from Iraq

I heaved a sigh of relief as the car pulled away from the airport, pleased to be at last on my way to my parents and away from the inquisitive media. I felt drained, yet wanted to talk about some of the things that we had experienced while we had been held hostage. So the Colonel got to hear quite a lot about our adventures in Kuwait and Iraq by the time he dropped us off at my parents' house. He said little, occasionally asking a question to clarify a point, but mainly keeping his eyes on the road, happy to let me tell of our experiences. The next day, however, he was back in London, and had a chance to tell the Queen some of our story and a little about the situations that we had all been through. This stood Her Majesty in good stead, as when the Prime Minister, Margaret Thatcher, came to see her twenty-four hours later, the Queen was ahead of the game and was able to give Mrs Thatcher snippets of information that the Prime Minister's officials were not privy to!

The reunion with Mum and Dad was fairly emotional for us all. They were waiting at the gate when the car pulled up, and I couldn't help noticing how much older they both looked. Obviously the stress and strain that our detainment had put on them had taken their toll. But that thought was put to one side as we scrambled out of the car, everyone laughing and talking at once and no one making much sense. The children were very excited to see Nana and Granddad again, especially Laura, whose prayer had been so dramatically answered. After getting our very sparse belongings out of the car, we said our goodbyes to the Colonel, and went into my parents' house for the first time in ages.

Soon the kettle was on the boil, and a lovely British cuppa was being enjoyed by us all. Although I had wanted to talk about our experiences to the Colonel, I hesitated to say too much to Mum and Dad. For one thing I was tired, but I also wanted to shield them from some of the nastier things that we had had to endure. I guessed there would be time for all that in due course.

Within ten minutes the children were out in the garden, playing with a ball, as though they had never been away. Even though they were having a good time, they were soon back in the house again. It was now early September, the weather was cool, and we had only the clothes that we wore in the hottest days in Iraq. I knew that we would soon have to go on a major shopping spree for clothes. But not today. I wasn't up to that. Mum noticed our predicament. 'You all look frozen to me,' she said, concern showing in her eyes. 'If we're not careful, you'll all go down with the flu. Come up to my room and I'll see what we can let you have to keep you warm.' The children bounded up the stairs, amused at the thought of trying on grown-up clothes. Mum opened up her chest of drawers, full of neatly folded cardigans and jumpers. We all laughed as Andrew put on a jumper belonging to my dad which all but drowned him, while Laura and I put on cardigans, although Mum was still looking concerned as she saw how chilled we felt.

We had arrived back on my sister's birthday. The family

had arranged a surprise party, but no one had anticipated just how much of a surprise party it was going to be! Even though we were all feeling tired after the flight, I reasoned that it would be a good way of seeing several family members as they gathered together for the party. So while Anne went to take the dog for a walk, completely oblivious of what was going on, Dad drove us over to her house where we hid, waiting for her return.

When she came back, we all jumped out on her, and her face was an absolute picture! Although we are not normally the kind of family that hugs each other a lot, today was an exception. We laughed and shed a few tears as we tried to catch up with all the news while tucking into the special birthday food that the family had provided. The time with Anne and the rest of the family was good, but in some ways it was also slightly unreal. Here I was, enjoying a birthday party in England, while Peter was still stuck in Iraq. I didn't want to spoil the time for the others, but I couldn't get rid of the feeling of sadness every time I thought about him.

When I got into bed that night after an evening of chatting, glimpsing ourselves returning to Heathrow on the evening news, and settling the children, I thought again about Peter and where he was. In the privacy of my bedroom the tears started to roll down my cheeks. I had pains in my chest and in my head. I felt rotten. Eventually I cried myself to sleep, wishing over and over that we hadn't had to be separated again after such a short period of time.

I woke again in the early hours of the morning. I couldn't get back to sleep, so I crept downstairs, prayed for a while, and then made myself a cup of tea. Mum must have heard me moving around, and came to see what was going on. I was sorry that she could see my distress, but maybe it was better that she knew how I was feeling. We talked for a while, and I began to realise afresh that I needed to put my feelings to one side, if for no other reason than to give the children some stability. 'You'll be fine when you've had some rest, love,' said Mum kindly. 'You've had an awful time, but you're safe now. I'd try and get back off to sleep if I were you. It's another big day tomorrow – or do I mean today?' she said, giving the clock an anxious glance.

Next day was Laura's eighth birthday. I had wondered what I could get her that would be special to her, but not too expensive for me. I was very aware that all the banking arrangements still had to be sorted out, as the banks had frozen virtually all of the accounts which were linked to Kuwait and Iraq.

The idea suddenly came to me to buy her a pet. I figured that it would be something that she could lavish her affection on, and would help take her mind off any of the events that might be causing her distress, although neither of the children showed any signs at all of being disturbed by the events that they had been through. So that is how Pip the hamster became part of the Barlow household. I also bought Andrew a football, as he didn't have any toys to play with, apart from the teddy and other bits and pieces that he had been given at the airport. I watched as Laura fussed over her new pet and Andrew dribbled the ball on Dad's back lawn. 'Thanks, Mum, they're great,' they said, as they continued to play. I felt pleased that they appreciated the little that I had been able to get for them. They were good kids. Peter would be proud of them, I thought, making a mental note to remember as much as I could to pass on to him next time we spoke.

After sorting out as much of the banking arrangements as I could, I went on a mad shopping trip for the clothes and other items that I needed. If anyone is thinking that, if they could plan their wardrobe from nothing, they would

127

not make the mistakes that they had in the past, I have something to tell them. Forget it! I found myself buying things which neither suited me nor fitted me very well, partly thanks to my lack of interest and partly because I am the same person who made the mistakes in the first place! I used to love shopping, but now I hated it with a vengeance. For this reason I was extremely grateful when Mary Stewart-Wilson came to visit, smiling broadly as she usually did, bearing gifts. She had phoned my mother asking for my clothes size, and now arrived with a complete outfit of clothes for me. She gave me a hug and said how sorry she was about my circumstances, pressing a bundle into my hands at the same time. This consisted of a very smart outfit consisting of skirt, blouse, shoes, tights and handbag. Troubles often bring out the best in people, and this was no exception. So many people gave me gifts of clothing and items to start our home up again. How touched and thankful I was to see this first-hand.

What did strike me as I went round the shops was the attitude of some of the people. They were walking around as though nothing was wrong, as though there wasn't a war still going on in Iraq. Of course, for them it had little or no impact on their lives, but I was keenly aware of every twist and turn, because of Peter's involvement. I passed one couple who were having a heated argument about which toothpaste to buy. I wanted to go up to them and tell them to stop quarrelling – didn't they know that my husband was being held hostage across the other side of the world? Sadly I walked away, head down, alone in my despair, realising that those around me were just getting on with everyday living as I had done such a short time ago.

I felt that it was important that the children had a regular routine now that they were back in their own country, and although I didn't know how long we would be with my parents, I went down to the local school and asked the headteacher if they could be taken on as pupils. This was agreed, and Andrew and Laura started the very next day. It was great to be with Mum and Dad, but we all knew it was only a short-term arrangement. We needed a home of our own, and to get on with our life again. The army offered us some quarters that I didn't really like, so I asked them for the quarters that we would have gone into at the end of our posting to Kuwait. Somewhat to my surprise they agreed, so three weeks after arriving in Britain we were on the move again, this time to Tidworth in Hampshire.

I felt at home as soon as I saw the pretty little three-bedroomed house, and even though I didn't know anyone in the area, the army was always there on hand to help. I was given a code word by them – *Operation Hastings* – which I was told to quote when ringing them up in need of anything, they would immediately know who I was and how to deal with my request. Lots of people came to call when I was in my new home, inviting me to go to their homes for coffee and a chat. Shyness held me back from accepting their well-meant invitations. One exception to that, though, was when Barbara, the padre's wife, came to call. Very tall, with lovely dark hair, she had a caring, thoughtful nature and was a born organiser. Her warm and friendly personality impressed me, and I felt that she was someone who I could genuinely trust. She and her husband Mike became good friends of mine, inviting me for meals at their home and for walks with their dog. I appreciated their friendship so much, and the kindness that they showed to me.

The telephone came into its own in my new situation. I would be constantly on the line to those that I had been with in Kuwait and Iraq, like my friend Jean. It was good to be able to relate to others who were in the same situation as me. The people who had been based in

Kuwait but were out of the country when the invasion took place were a wonderful supportive help to us all. I was learning afresh how important friendship was. A support group was formed through Barbara's endeavours for the families whose men were going out to Saudi. I got involved and helped organise some coffee mornings, when the military would come in and talk to the wives, explaining the latest situation to them. I'm sure that relating to this group, rather than just concentrating totally on my own situation, actually helped me.

Soon after I had returned from the Gulf, an army official paid me a visit, to interview me about what I had seen during my time out there. I was asked about tanks, military installations and aircraft. I had always thought myself to be a fairly observant person, but trying to distinguish between one army vehicle and the next turned out to be a weak point of mine! I found the process of having to answer a long list of questions stressful, even though I knew they had to find out as much as they could. I was able to tell them quite accurately where our husbands were being held, because of the map that we had had with us. I sometimes worried that now they knew exactly where the important installations were, they would know exactly where to bomb.

Just as I was unlocking the front door one windy Friday, loaded up with groceries, I heard the phone start to ring. I got to it just before the caller decided to put the phone down. It was the army to say that a meeting had been arranged for a few days hence at Bagshot Park for all the women who were caught up in the Gulf drama. I was told it would give us up-to-the-minute details on where our husbands were and the role that the British Embassy were playing, as well as letting us know about the help that we could get.

The day soon arrived, and a military car came to pick me up for my overnight stay. Dad carried my little case to the car, as I gave last-minute instructions to Mum about bedtimes and food likes and dislikes as far as the children were concerned. 'Don't worry about a thing,' said Mum, patting me on the shoulder. 'The children will be fine. You just go and have a nice time with your friends. I'll have a meal waiting when you get back.'

With a final wave, I found myself being whisked off in the car. It didn't seem long before I arrived at Bagshot Park, a very large and beautiful building set in the most marvellous grounds, full of mature trees and flowering plants. I joined the women already gathering in the main lounge for a cup of coffee. I was pleased to see so many familiar faces. Jean entered soon after me, smiling as she walked across the room to pick up a cup of coffee. To be among women who were experiencing many of the emotions that troubled me was comforting. It was therefore upsetting for us all when our conversations were interrupted by an official of some sort requesting we look on a board to find our names and next to them a room number we should proceed to.

I was ushered into a very imposing room, where the chairs had been arranged in a wide circle. There were about a dozen or so women there, most of whom I recognised, although I didn't know any of them particularly well. I looked round for Jean, but she was nowhere to be seen. A man sat in the middle of the circle, who I guess must have been a psychologist or psychiatrist. Without any preamble, he started to fire questions at us. How did we feel when Kuwait was attacked, he wanted to know. Everyone started to look awkward as they tried to put into words their innermost feelings during such a vulnerable time of their lives.

I could understand the army's interest in us as a group. We were, after all, the first people who had ever been held as hostages in a modern war situation. Normally, when a war breaks out, all the people who are not involved in it, all the expats and foreigners, are immediately evacuated. So I figured the army were keen to learn all they could about our reactions. But the way they chose to do it badly backfired. The questions that the man was firing at us demanded a personal response, and none of us felt like opening up all our private thoughts and emotions in front of a group of relative strangers. An embarrassed silence hung over the room as the counsellor tried his best to coax some information out of us. A large proportion of the women, including me, suddenly took a great interest in our shoes and the carpet design rather than looking directly at our inquisitor, for fear of risking being asked a question! By the time lunchtime came we had had enough, and although an afternoon session was planned, most of us opted out. Maybe the army needed information and maybe we needed help with the stress that we had experienced, but this was definitely not the way to go about it. Chatting to Jean over lunch, I learnt that much the same kind of situation prevailed at her session too. It was good to spend some time with her again, and other friends. Everyone agreed that being together, catching up with the other members of the group and talking among ourselves had been more beneficial than anything that the army had tried to lay on for us!

Late that afternoon we were told that an information meeting had been arranged for us. This meeting we *did* appreciate. We were told the military build-up in the Gulf, and the latest news on our husbands – that they were well, and as far as was known were not being ill-treated. We were offered help to sort out banking problems and were assured that we would be receiving our husbands' pay as long as the conflict continued.

Although it was generally agreed that the time at Bagshot Park was not a success, the army need to be given credit for trying to help in the best way that they could. A further meeting was arranged a little while later, when the children were invited to go along. This meeting was attended by Tom King, Margaret Thatcher's Defence Minister at the time. Arriving in a helicopter, much to the excitement and delight of the kids, he talked to us about the Government's policy on the Gulf War. Counsellors were again on hand, this time for private sessions if required. I did not take up the offer. The consensus among the women at this gathering was that, although the army was doing all that it could, there was a distinct possibility that our husbands would not return.

I found myself praying – and crying – every night for Peter. I probably did as much of one as the other. Most nights I fell asleep crying, only to wake up in the early hours, still with the situation heavy on my mind. The children, on the other hand, seemed to be taking the situation in their stride. If they knew of my distress they never showed it, and did all the normal things that school kids do, including misbehaving from time to time. Friends became even more important and special, as they showed such kindness to me by inviting me over to their homes for a meal, or buying me something special, like an item of clothing. Their thoughtfulness was very touching.

I started to go to the local garrison church, where Barbara's husband Mike was one of the padres. There was so much love shown to me by the people who attended, and I particularly appreciated the prayers said for our family each week. After a little while a prayer meeting was organised each Tuesday morning especially for people caught up in the Gulf situation, which I attended, along with two or three others. I wanted to pray out loud, like the others, but I couldn't. I didn't know how to! So I just sat and listened, grateful for the prayers that were being said for us all.

November came, and with it the annual Service of Remembrance. It had been decided that year to centre the service around the soldiers who had gone out to Saudi and who were positioned on the border, waiting for things to develop. I went to the service on my own, leaving the children at home with Mum and Dad, who had come up for the weekend to help out. The church was packed, and I took my place alongside people I did not know, but who I guessed were local dignitaries in the town. During the course of the service they read out, among others, Peter's name, because he was one of the hostages, and then a few moments later they started to play the Last Post. Hearing Peter's name read out in church was one thing, but coupled with the mournful strains of the Last Post it was more than I could take. Tears started to course down my face, in spite of my best efforts to hold myself together. The lady next to me put a friendly arm around my shoulder – then she started to cry too! I found out later to my embarrassment that she was the local health visitor. I felt sure that she must have put me down as a case that needed watching!

A short time after that, I received an invitation to spend a weekend with some good friends of ours, Christine and Robin, and their two children, Chloe and Josie. I felt that it was going to be a special weekend, as I knew we all got on well together, our children and theirs referring to each other as cousins, as they had known each other since they were all tiny. When we set off to their house that Saturday morning though, there was nothing to give me any clue as to how special that weekend was going to be.

We were given a warm welcome by everyone, Robin making a special fuss of Andrew and Laura while I went into the kitchen to talk to Christine as the kettle boiled for a cup of tea. It was lovely to be with them again, and I tried to concentrate on the warmth of our friendship, rather than the fact that Peter was not around. After lunch, Robin had planned an activity with the children, which left Christine and me free to go to the shops. We spent a pleasant couple of hours wandering around the town, watching the early Christmas shoppers as they darted from one place to the next.

All too soon it was time to head home. It was obvious from the smiling faces that greeted us that the children had had a great time with Robin. Christine was just about to put the kettle on again when the phone rang. It was Mum. I had of course given her Robin and Christine's number so she could contact us should she need to.

'Sheila,' she said in an excited voice, 'Sheila, I've just been speaking to Peter on the phone!'

I felt my legs going weak, but in a surprisingly calm voice said, 'Mum, was he all right? Where was he phoning from? What did he say?'

Mum said that she had almost dropped the phone in shock when she answered it and heard Peter's voice on the line saying, 'Hello, Mother-in-law! How are you?' It turned out that because the Iraqi authorities wanted the men to encourage their wives to return to Iraq for Christmas, they had decided to let the men make a phone call home. Peter had no idea where I was living, as none of the letters that we had sent out to him had got through, but he had remembered my mum's phone number, which was just about the only one he knew by heart. She had told Peter that we were with Christine and Robin for the weekend, and had given him their number. He said that he would be able to ring later that day.

About an hour later the phone rang, and I found myself talking to Peter long-distance from Iraq. Words can't say how wonderful it was to hear his voice, and to be able to speak to him again. But Peter, being Peter, quickly took control of the conversation, wanting to know how we all were, how we were managing financially, how the children were, where we were living and so on. There were so many things that quite naturally he wanted to know. He told me that all the men had been listening to the World Service when we had been travelling back to the UK, and they had let out a cheer when it had been announced that we had returned home safely. We chatted for a while longer, and all too soon the telephone time ended. But before he rang off, he said that the Iraqi authorities were inviting us to all go back for Christmas. I knew by the tone of his voice and the way he was speaking that, although that was what the Iraqis wanted, it was certainly not a wish that he had, although he couldn't say so directly. He nattered on the phone to the children for a few moments, telling them that he would hopefully be home soon, and to be good for Mum in the meantime!

After I eventually put the phone down on Peter I wondered when I would speak to him again. But I was to discover that this was no one-off event. I started to get a phone call from him practically every day, with sometimes a gap of a day or two in between. He was always very up-beat and positive, and I was always the same when he rang.

The other wives were getting calls from their husbands, too, including Jean, although for her the situation was complicated by the fact that she now had a part-time office job and therefore was not always in the right place when Sean rang. So I would occasionally pass on messages to her from him, via Peter. We had become good friends, and we did all that we could to help each other.

We needed all the support we could get with Christmas approaching and no sign of our husbands' release. I determined to make it as happy a time as I could, in spite of my inner sadness, for the sake of the children. Being gloomy wasn't going to help anyone, I decided. As tough as our situation was, we were aware of others who were suffering far more. News had reached us that following a trip that Edward Heath had made to Iraq, Saddam had declared an amnesty to any young foreign students still in hiding in Kuwait. Colonel Duncan, who had been so helpful to us in the early days of the invasion, putting his and his family's life at risk in ringing us with up-to-the-minute information, was still in hiding with his two sons, Rory and Alex. When the amnesty was announced, his two sons came out of hiding and were driven to the airport by two Iraqi drivers. Sadly they were involved in a car crash, and Alex was killed, while Rory sustained quite a bad injury to his back. At that point Colonel Duncan also came out of hiding, and was allowed to fly home with Rory and the body of Alex. A funeral service was held at his former college, and quite a few of the Liaison Team attended the funeral. I felt so sad for Bruce and Toni. As the service commenced, I reflected on how awful war is, and how it strikes out and hurts so many people's lives. How many more tears would be shed before this conflict was over? The unanswered question continued to occupy my thoughts as the final hymn was announced. How I wished we could put the clock back six months and alter that part of history.

14

Prayer and Praise

I received a letter from the army a few days later, asking me to list all the things that we had lost in Kuwait at the time of the invasion. They wanted me to list every single item that we had, from a teaspoon to the family car, including how many pairs of socks we all had, how many photo albums, what ornaments we possessed, and the amount and cost of the children's toys! I found this task completely daunting. I half-heartedly went through an Argos catalogue, trying to remember all the things in our house and what they had cost at the time we bought them, but frankly my heart just wasn't in it at all. Rightly or wrongly I didn't care what we had lost financially, I just wanted us all to be together again as a family. Our insurance company had said that none of our policies would be honoured, but the army said that they would try and help us out. I know I should have felt more grateful, but it all seemed so trivial compared to the greater loss of not having Peter with me.

His phone calls continued, with the conversations between us getting more cryptic by the day. We would talk about 'the family' when we meant the regiment, and had an everyday phrase for each army term we wanted to talk about. Sometimes the conversation was so cryptic that at the end of it, I wasn't sure what we had said to each other!

One bit of news that I managed to tell him, in code, was that he had now been made an officer, which made me feel very proud of him. Army life continued even in captivity!

By the beginning of December I was beginning to feel confused in my own mind about whether I should be going back to be with Peter for Christmas. Some wives had already flown out, and then returned with their husbands. One part of me said that was probably because the men were sick anyway, but another part questioned whether I was doing everything I could to help Peter's release. I shared my thoughts about returning with Mum and Dad, who hit the roof, telling me how much the children needed me, saying in no uncertain terms that one parent was better than none, and that they were far too old to take responsibility for Andrew and Laura if for any reason I was detained again. I saw the fear in Dad's eyes which came out in an angry outburst of words, and knew that they were worried about what I might do.

Although I knew they were right to feel concerned, I still went ahead and made provisional plans to return. I asked our good friends Robin and Christine if they would look after the children if I decided to go back, which they agreed to do, and I asked Barbara if she would take me to the airport, should I need to go. I also made arrangements to get a temporary passport. I spoke to Jean on the phone, voicing my thoughts that I might go back, which I know caused her some concern and confusion as to what her correct role should be.

Headaches and pains in my chest now seemed to be a daily occurrence. I was still crying myself to sleep every night, when no one was around to see how much I was hurting. It was the first week in December, and as I crawled into bed after another day of missing Peter and doubts about what I should be doing, I started to feel that I couldn't go on much longer the way I was. My head hurt so much it felt as though it was going to explode inside my skull, and I felt totally miserable and pressurised. After a long time of crying, I suddenly found myself praying. But it wasn't the nice structured prayers that I had read out loud at the Anglican church, or even the sincere prayers that I had heard others pray and wished I could copy at the prayer meetings I had attended. This was a raw, heartfelt prayer from the very depth of my being, and I was praying for me! Not for my husband, not for my children, not for my country, but for me. It was me who was falling apart, it was me who didn't know what to do, it was me needing help.

There were no structured sentences or nice phrases, just an anguished prayer from the heart. The words came rushing out of me in torrents. If there was a God in heaven, He couldn't help but hear, even if He chose not to answer. I knew I was sinking fast, and I cried out, just as a drowning person would. Gradually my prayer subsided, and I eventually drifted off into a fitful sleep.

I woke the next morning feeling . . . dreadful! My head hurt, and so did my body. I felt that I was cracking up, and didn't know where to turn. But as always life had to go on. I got up, had a shower, got dressed and put on a pleasant smile for the kids while I prepared their breakfast. After they had left for school, I decided I couldn't stay in the house on my own – I had to get out for a while. I went into town, buying a few bits and pieces before ending up in a little gift shop, thinking that I might spot something or other for stocking gifts. The jolly music that came from a portable radio tuned to Radio 2 grated with my thoughts, and I tried to block out the cheerful sounds which were such an intrusion into the hurt that I was feeling.

Suddenly I was aware of a voice on the radio that I recognised. It was a woman called Sue. She was an expat whose husband was working with computers at the time of the invasion. She was speaking at the end of the brief hourly news bulletin. I just caught her saying to the interviewer, 'Well, if that is true, there will be dancing in the streets!' If what were true? Had something happened that I hadn't been told about? I rushed past all the baubles and glitter in the shop, and back to the car. I raced home, feeling certain that something was going on that I needed to know about!

As I parked the car on the drive, my next-door neighbour, home for his lunch break, dashed out of his house and said, 'Great news, Sheila! Have you heard?'

'Heard what?' I said in frustration. 'What's going on?'

'Saddam Hussein has announced that all the hostages are to be released, and they'll all be home for Christmas,' he said excitedly. 'I'm so pleased for you, Sheila.'

Deep in thought, I thanked him with hardly a smile on my face, and unlocked the front door, trying to work out what was going on. If it were true, it would be wonderful, but if this was just a false alarm . . . Why should he let them go? What would he be gaining? He would lose all his bargaining power, and his military installations would be at great risk. Why should it happen now? My thoughts were racing. Then I suddenly remembered my anguished prayers of the night before. I had told God in no uncertain terms that I was at the end of my tether, I couldn't go on, He would have to do something. And here I was, a few hours later, hearing that the whole thing was coming to an end. Was it a big coincidence, or had God really heard and answered my prayer?

The question was still hanging in my mind when the phone started to ring. It was Mum, wondering if I had heard the news. What did I think? We chatted for a while, with me saying things which I am sure didn't make much sense. The call ended, and I turned on the TV. The news was full of the announcement. A few more calls came through from friends sending their love and support. I rang Jean at work, and wanted to hear her comments. 'Sheila, I'd love to think that it was true, but I just don't think we ought to get too excited. It might be a way of trying to get us all back to Iraq again – and yet everyone seems to think they will be released . . .' she said, her voice trailing off. We agreed to keep in touch, and I decided not to get over-confident or over-excited.

The children came home, and I of course had to mention it to them, but did so in a guarded way.

'I heard on the news that Saddam has said that the hostages might be released soon, but I think we shouldn't take too much notice of it, until we hear a bit more,' I said matter of factly.

They nodded in agreement, and said 'Oh great,' but soon the conversation turned to what homework they had, and what I had made for tea. I was pleased that they hadn't got too excited. It would be awful to have their hopes dashed so close to Christmas. It did spur us on, though, to think about putting up the Christmas tree!

Peter rang later that evening. He had heard the announcement on the World Service, but he had not been told anything about it officially.

'Don't let your hopes get too high, luv,' I heard him say down the phone, the line emphasising his northern accent. 'If it's going to happen, it'll happen right enough.' He was correct of course, but I decided the next morning that in case it turned out to be true, I had better do a little preparation. I went out shopping again, this time for underwear and shirts, and one or two odds and ends, so he would have something to wear when he first came home before building up his own wardrobe again.

Harry, who had become a close friend of Peter's, rang from America. He had been moved into the camp after we had left to return home along with three Frenchmen and a German, and had been held for a short time with Peter. The two men had got on very well together, sharing their hearts and their morning jog. Harry was very excited about the announcement that had been made by Saddam, and promised to let me know what he heard from his side of the Atlantic.

Barbara rang, and invited us all out for a walk with her dog Centre. It sounded like a good idea – we needed to get out of the house and have a bit of a blow in the fresh air. Joining us was Cilla, another friend of Barbara's who also had a dog. Cilla was due to have her first baby in a few days' time, and was in a joyful mood in anticipation of this happy event. We all set off over the hills, enjoying the fresh air and each other's company.

It was dark by the time we returned, and the little red light on my answerphone was flashing impatiently to be acknowledged. It was Peter's voice I heard when I pressed the play button, saying that he was being moved again, within the next fifteen minutes. 'I'll try and ring again as soon as I can, Sheila,' he said, adding, 'I suppose it could mean that the rumour about us coming home is true, but don't build your hopes too high. Love you,' he said, before ending the call. Could it indeed be what we had all been waiting for, I wondered, as I pressed the replay button to hear his message again.

The next day brought more news of preparations for the men coming home. Harry rang again to say that news was coming through on American TV that an aeroplane was about to take off in Iraq, full of Western hostages, but that no details of exactly who was on the plane had been released. He promised to keep me informed. This was getting pretty exciting, and my hopes started to be raised, in spite of Peter's warnings and my better judgment.

There was no way I was going to leave the house, in case I missed a vital phone call, but I knew that I had to keep myself occupied. I decided that it would be a good idea to put up a few balloons and a welcome home message – just in case it turned out to be true. I had, in the best traditions of the Perry Como song, tied a yellow ribbon round a tree in the garden a week or so before, and I also had a yellow ribbon tied to our car radio aerial. I phoned Barbara to ask if she knew where I could get some bunting, and she told me that she had some that I could have, and she would bring it over. Meanwhile, Cilla, our mutual friend, had just started to go into labour, so Barbara brought the bunting over in the car with Cilla in the back. It was good to see her, and I gave her a hug and wished her well before she sped off to the hospital with Barbara. Soon the outside of the house was festooned with balloons, bunting and bits of coloured paper. I wondered what the neighbours were going to think, as some didn't even realise that I was involved in the hostage crisis.

The phone rang constantly as friends tried to get the latest information from me. Harry came on the line again. 'News is just coming through that the plane I was telling you about earlier has now left Iraq for Gatwick,' he said. Replacing the receiver, I jumped as it immediately shrilled out again. This time it was John, one of our friends who was manning the army help-line. His broad Scottish accent made me concentrate carefully on what he was saying. 'Sheila, have you heard that a plane is in the air carrying hostages home from Iraq? There are still no details about who exactly is on board, but my advice is that you get to the airport – just in case. I reckon there is a good chance Peter is on board.'

He didn't need to repeat his advice – in my mind I was already on the way – but I was in no fit state to drive. I was shaking too much! A quick ring to Robin fixed the transport problem, and he readily agreed to drive me to the airport, even though he lived an hour's drive away. Then I rang the school to ask for permission to take the children out. They would never have forgiven me if they had missed out on this. By now I was feeling more and more certain that this really was the day we had been waiting so long for. The school secretary was very kind, and made arrangements for me to go in and pick them up. Soon they were back home and eating a quickly prepared sandwich, while waiting for Robin to arrive and take us to the airport.

At last I spied Robin's pale metallic blue car turn into the end of the road. I shouted to the children, and before he had time to turn the car round we were out of the house and waiting on the kerb. As we all scrambled into the car, I turned to look at the house once more. I thought for a moment how awful it would be if we came back to this highly decorated house without Peter! I pushed these negative thoughts to the back of my mind as we started our journey to Gatwick Airport.

As we proceeded on the journey, I wondered what the returning hostages would be thinking and observing as they flew back into Britain. I remembered how struck I had been by the green fields and hedges of England after the dry sandy landscape of Iraq and Kuwait, and wondered if they would notice that too. Eventually we arrived at the airport, and I couldn't help noticing the outside broadcast vans of the BBC, ITV and Sky News. They obviously thought it was worth their while being here this evening, I thought ruefully. Not long now and we would all know what was going on.

Robin dropped us at the main entrance, and said that he would go and park the car and then get a bite to eat before joining us again later on. I walked through the airport with Andrew and Laura, trying to spot any familiar faces. I caught sight of an information desk, went up to the smartly dressed official, and explained why I was there. He was most helpful and explained that all the families and friends of the returning hostages were being asked to go to another part of the airport. He gave me the number of the room to go to.

'There is a list in that room of all the people who are on tonight's flight,' he said. 'You'd best make sure that your husband's name is on it, Madam,' he said politely, adding with a smile 'Good luck.'

I was soon in the vicinity of the room which contained that all-important list. A long queue had formed of people like me eager to learn news of their loved ones. I spotted several people I knew waiting for information further up the queue, and we waved at each other, sensing how we were all feeling. Nicky was there, and after finding that her husband's name was on the list came to tell us that she had heard that everyone from the British Liaison Team was on the plane. I wanted to believe that so much, but just like doubting Thomas, until I saw Peter with my own eyes I couldn't truly believe!

As we got nearer the head of the queue I found my heart beating faster. Finally I was facing the woman who was checking each name given to her. I gave Peter's name, knowing that she would not have to look through too much of the list as our surname begins with B. It only took her a few moments to check the list, although it seemed like minutes, and yes, she confirmed that his name was there. He really was on his way home!

I hugged the children, who were jumping up and down

146

with excitement. It almost seemed too good to be true. We thanked the woman, and made a quick exit, partly to let other people have their loved one's name checked, and partly to see who of our friends we could spot in the waiting room. A Sky News team was filming, and they stopped me and asked if I was one of the women waiting for their husbands to come home.

'Yes,' I said excitedly, 'I've just been told he is definitely on the plane coming in tonight.'

'Would you mind saying a few words for tonight's news programme please?' said the reporter, and before I knew it I was gabbling away about the whole situation. I have no idea what I said, I felt so excited, but no doubt it all went out on a Sky News broadcast, although I never saw it.

I was very pleased to see Jean, who was as excited as I was. Her two children were with her, and there was lots of happy chatter as families waited for the plane to arrive. Jean wanted to know all the latest, even though we had chatted on the phone just a little while before. I told her about my highly decorated house, and we laughed, relieved that we were coming to the end of so much tension and anxiety.

Then I spotted Peter's family. There was his sister Julie and her husband Michael, chatting to Peter's brother Paul and his wife Denise. It was good to see them, and to catch up on how they had been coping. We still had about two hours to wait before the plane was due, and the room we were now in was very cramped.

Why is it that time goes so slowly when you want something good to happen? Every few moments I looked at my watch, only to see that it had hardly moved at all. But even the most stubborn of clocks has to yield to the tides of time, and eventually an announcement was made that the flight we had all been waiting for was now approaching the airport. We were then ushered into a slightly larger room. All eyes were focused on the double doors through which, we were told, the men would come. The atmosphere was now lighthearted but tense, with people chatting in small groups, realising that they didn't have much longer to wait before their husbands, brothers or sons would be with them once more.

Stewards came and opened the doors, and most of the chatter stopped as we waited for the first of the men to appear. A cheer went up as it was announced that the plane had landed and the men were disembarking, and then, a few minutes later, the first of the men appeared. Another cheer went up, as people ran towards them, laughing and crying and hugging each other. Each time the next man appeared someone would shout out his name, and all his relatives would rush up and surround him.

Then I heard another great cheer, and I heard someone shout, 'Peter Barlow – Peter Barlow is here!' and suddenly there was Peter, looking thinner than when I had last seen him. His usually short and tidy haircut had grown longer, and I noticed that some of his hair was still ruffled from the long flight. His family thoughtfully stood back for a few moments while the children and I rushed up to him, hugging and kissing him. Everything around us melted into a blur as we shared this precious moment with each other. It was so wonderful to see him again. We were back together as a family. The nightmare was over. I could never have guessed, as I felt Peter's strong arms around me once more, that, for me at least, another nightmare was just about to begin.

15

More Pain – Some Gain

It was good that some of Peter's close family members were there to hear first-hand his latest news, and to see him looking fit and well, although slightly tired. Peter was also grateful to those who had been able to make the trip to the airport. Not only did he want to hear all our news, but he also wanted to find out how his brother and sisters and their respective families had fared during his time away. But eventually it was time to head in our various directions. Robin had promised to ferry us back home. After saying our goodbyes, and pushing past the press, we all scrambled into Robin's car. I was feeling thankful that I didn't have to get behind the wheel and drive us all home after such an emotional time.

Peter could have had no doubt which was our house as we rounded the corner which led into our street. Some of the balloons decorating the house had burst, but there were still enough to make a vivid splash of colour against the grey morning light. The car stopped at the kerb, and we all piled out, feeling stiff and tired. Although Robin and Peter were not normally demonstrative towards each other, they gave each other a quick bear hug, Robin pushing a bottle of champagne into Peter's hands before saying his final goodbyes and making his way back home. It was now five o'clock in the morning, and we were all tired beyond belief. I promised the children a day off from school. With the best will in the world, they couldn't have gone anyway.

They were both excited to have Peter home, and grabbing him by the hand gave him a tour of the house, all conducted at breakneck speed accompanied by lots of happy laughter. They showed him the sitting room and our new TV, then the kitchen, pointing out the new washing machine, standing white and gleaming in the corner. Next it was their bedrooms, and then our bedroom. They were delighted at his bewilderment as he tried to take it all in.

After a few hours of snatched sleep we were up again. It was Tuesday, the day that the prayer group met to pray for the hostages like Peter who were caught up in the conflict, and also for the soldiers who were in Saudi, waiting to get the Iraqis out of Kuwait. So there was no way we could stay in bed, as much as we wanted to.

Peter made a few phone calls while I organised a light breakfast of tea and toast. He had started to help but soon gave up. He seemed to be opening every cupboard to find basics like teacups and spoons, and eventually left me to it. The problems continued when he decided to change into a new set of clothes. I had sorted out all the clothing that I had bought for him and put it away in drawers and the wardrobe, but he had to ask me where everything was, which was a slight source of irritation for him.

More problems were to follow. He didn't know anyone in the street where we now lived, and likewise all the people in our church were new to him. For him everything was strange, but familiar to me. Always in the past he had been the one to make contact with people first, breaking the ice for me. Now I was the one to make the introductions, and give Peter information about the area in which we lived.

The next few days were spent adjusting as a family. When

I took the children back to school I was given a card and a bottle of sherry from their teachers, which showed such kindness on their part. People who I did not know very well and Peter had never met would stop us in the street and say how pleased they were that Peter was back home. We were touched by the care and concern that was being shown to us.

At home, though, the relationship between Peter and me was strained. I had longed for Peter to come home – it seemed to have been my one prevailing thought for months. Now he was home, however, it wasn't the idyllic time that I had imagined it would be. Although Peter had not suffered undue stress during his captivity, because he had been confident that he would eventually be released, the tension of living in a confined area with the other men was now telling on him, especially as it seemed as though he was superfluous in his own home. I had arranged the furniture in our new house the way I wanted it, I was paying the bills and making the running in all things, simply because I had had to while he was away. I was pleased that things were ticking over nicely, but it must have made Peter feel like a spare part, and he was soon ready to criticise anything that he uncovered that he felt I hadn't handled well.

Several letters had come in while he had been away, which didn't demand an immediate reply. I had put them in the top drawer of the bureau (the drawer he would have normally claimed) to be answered when I had more time. He found the letters, along with a few other odds and ends, and told me off for not dealing with them. I bit my lip, wanting to defend my action, or lack of it, but not wanting to start an argument. A little while later he came across the claim that I had been asked to make by the army for the things we had lost in Kuwait. At the time I was asked

151

to submit it I didn't know or care what anything cost, or what it was now worth. Everything seemed unimportant against the main concern of getting Peter freed. But when Peter saw the figures I had submitted he exploded, saying that I had vastly underestimated the value of the things we had lost, and that other wives had submitted far more realistic claims.

I felt hurt and angry. Where was this wonderful reunion that I had longed for, I thought bitterly. All I seemed to be doing was defending my actions all the time, and I had to give an account for all my movements. At least when Peter was away I could go for a walk with Barbara or one of my other friends if I wanted to. Now I had to think what Peter might want to do. A cloud seem to descend on our marriage.

Then Peter started to get irritable with the children. Their bedrooms, although never totally messy, were often less tidy than their father liked them to be, and he told them off, making them feel wary of him in spite of the fact that they were glad to see him home. We were all walking on eggshells, wondering when the next explosion would occur.

The truth was that Peter had to find his role in the family again. What should have been the best time of our married life turned out to be the worst, with conversations very often resulting in arguments. I frequently found myself in tears, wondering just what was going on. For the first time in my marriage I felt like walking out. I am sure that at this time I was ultra-sensitive, having suddenly gone from living every day fearful for my husband's life to euphoria that he was safe, all in such a short space of time. Emotionally I was drained, physically I was exhausted. No wonder Peter and I had such difficulty readjusting to life together. Peter needed to regain his role as head of the household, and I just wanted a peaceful life! But the commitment that we had made to each other on our wedding day stood firm, and gradually our relationship started to get back on a more even keel, much to everyone's relief. Peter settled down in his new job as Families Officer for the regiment, the children settled back into school and life rolled on.

I was grateful that the period of time we spent as hostages seemed to have had little effect on the children. When I asked them what they remembered about Kuwait, Andrew would mention the sea and the fish market, and Laura would mention learning to swim. When I asked them later what they remembered about the time when Kuwait was invaded, and all the upheaval that we went through, Andrew remembered the scorpion-in-the-jar incident, while Laura remembered the wonderful food we had in the hotel, and playing with Jean's children. They never made reference to some of the more unpleasant things that we had to go through, which surprised and pleased me.

At the end of January 1991 all the military and their wives who had been stationed in Kuwait during the time of the invasion were invited to attend a meeting at RAF Uxbridge. This was partly to answer outstanding questions and also to reunite us with the other members of the team in a relaxed atmosphere.

A lovely surprise that stemmed from this concerned an American lady who had spent a short while in the camp where we had been living at the start of the invasion. After we had evacuated the camp, she, along with lots of others, had been moved in by the Iraqis to take our places a few days later. What she found when she arrived was much devastation, with many of our personal possessions thrown around. Going by the writing, pictures and dates of events that we had drawn on the walls, she realised some of what we had been through. This saddened and touched her and she decided to make it her responsibility to collate as many photographs as she could gather, along with any other important documents still recognisable, and get them back to the right families. We were told that this took many painstaking weeks, but she did a wonderful job. One of her successes was a family portrait of the four of us taken just before the invasion. It was the only item of ours that made it through the war, so we value it greatly. We will always be grateful to that wonderful lady who cared enough for strangers to go out of her way to do that for us. The picture was returned via the British Embassy and eventually given back to us at this meeting in Uxbridge.

Peter's homecoming made me assess my own life. I felt that I needed to move on, to grow up in some ways, I suppose. I felt that I still had a lot to learn, not least about things spiritual. I wanted to know how to study the Bible, but because of my own pride hesitated to ask anyone's advice. So I would start to read from the beginning, as I had in previous times, and then give up after a while. I didn't really know where to find anything in the Bible, either. If I was in a Bible study and we were asked to turn to a particular book, I watched where others were turning, then turned to the same point in my Bible and would try and find the passage from there. My foolish pride held me back from looking in the index, as I did not want to stand out as different from the rest of the group. Praying out loud was also a barrier that I just couldn't push through, no matter how hard I tried. Now that we were back in Britain I actually found myself praying less. With the crisis over there seemed less urgency to spend time praying, although I felt guilty about that.

I felt that I needed something positive to occupy my time. Then I heard about a typing course that was starting, and decided to go on it. To my surprise I enjoyed it, and so when a free space came on a computer course a few weeks later, I joined the course, and made good progress, to the delight of both myself and my tutor.

All our difficulties seemed to be behind us as June came. The relationship between Peter and me was good, his job was going well, and the children were happy at school. Laura had started riding lessons, and we got a little puppy, which we called Willow, to join the family. I was thinking about these things as I got the children's breakfast ready one morning, enjoying the warm sunshine streaming through the kitchen window, when I heard the familiar 'plop' of letters falling on to the doormat. Andrew and Laura rushed into the hall to see who could pick up the post first, and came dashing back with a couple of letters each.

One of the envelopes that Laura handed me stood out from the rest. It was a creamy colour, with the royal crest stamped on it instead of the normal postage stamp. I wondered what could possibly be inside and reasoned that there was only one way to find out! I took a knife from the drawer and carefully slit open the envelope, instead of ripping it open as I normally did with the mail that I received. I pulled out a stiff white card, with a gold royal crest at the top. I sat down at the kitchen table as I read out the words that were printed on it. It said

The Lord Chamberlain is
commanded by Her Majesty to invite
Mr and Mrs Peter Barlow
to a Garden Party at Buckingham Palace
on Tuesday 9th July 1991 from 4 until 6 p.m.

Morning Dress, uniform or lounge suit.

I read it, then reread it. Could this be so? An invitation to Buckingham Palace, no less! I rang up Peter with the news, and then rang up Mum. I don't know who was more delighted. We were all strong supporters of the Royal Family, and this was a great honour. But after the initial delight, panic set in. I had nothing to wear! It was all right for Peter, he could go in his uniform, but I would have to get a new outfit, there was no doubt about that!

I rang up Christine, my friend who I had known since my days as a nanny. It was through Christine that I had met Peter, who had been Christine and Robin's best man. They now lived in Warminster. She invited me over, in order that we could shop together for a special outfit for the occasion. We caught the train to Bath and must have visited every dress shop in the town, but nothing seemed to be right. Because I am small in stature, most of the outfits seemed to make me look dumpy or overweight. I was just about to give up when I spotted what seemed to be the ideal outfit in a little dress shop that we had almost overlooked. It was a white suit, made of linen material, with pink, blue and orange flowers on it, all set off with a green trim. A few days later I managed to find shoes and handbag to match, and I bought the first hat that I tried on. It perched on my head like a pill box, and I feared that it would fall off if I moved too quickly, but reckoned that it would be OK as long as I stood still in one place!

About a week after our invitation from the Queen had arrived, we received another exciting piece of mail. This was a letter from Colonel Stewart-Wilson. He had heard that Peter and I had been invited to the Garden Party, and was writing to invite us to meet him in the private section of the Palace, before the Garden Party started. He said that he would show us parts of the Palace that the general public would not normally see, including some of the priceless pictures that the Queen had in her collection! This made the day even more exciting, and we both looked forward to it with great anticipation.

The day duly arrived. We dressed in all our finery, and along with two other couples set out for the Palace, explaining to them that when we arrived we had a private appointment before the Garden Party began. Not wanting to be late for such an important occasion, we arrived with at least half an hour to spare. The area around the Palace was already bustling, with tourists staring through the railings at the guards in their sentry boxes, while other people, who had obviously been invited, were already showing their passes and going in. We had been told that no cameras were allowed inside the Palace, but there were photographers on hand outside who would take one's photograph – for a price! Peter and I lined up for a photograph, Peter looking extremely smart in his uniform, and me feeling anxious about my hat!

We showed our passes to the attendant, and found ourselves inside the railings. We decided to kill some time by walking the length of the building. As we walked past the first sentry box, the soldiers, recognising Peter's rank and uniform, snapped to attention and saluted, at the same time putting their guns over their shoulders and stamping their feet. Peter, looking slightly embarrassed, saluted them, then walked on to the next sentry box where the same thing happened. I wanted to giggle as I realised that this was going to happen each time we approached a sentry box. Finally the last one had been passed – only for us to realise with embarrassment that we had to walk past them all again to get back to where we needed to go! The crowds looking on must have thought we were really important people, with all the saluting and foot-stamping that we generated, but nothing could have been further from the truth.

When we finally met up with the Colonel, he had a surprise in store. With a twinkle in his eye he announced that someone had asked to have a word with us.

'Not the Queen?' I said, joking.

'Yes, as a matter of fact it is,' he said, smiling broadly. He told us that he had been able to relate some of our experiences to Her Majesty, and she had remarked that she would like a personal word with us, at the start of the Garden Party.

We didn't know what to think. I suddenly felt panicky. I wished I had spent the last four weeks practising my curtsey! We wanted to know how to address the sovereign, and what to do. The Colonel was marvellous, and put us at our ease, letting us know just what to say and how to say it.

The tour of the Palace started, as promised. I am sure that we must have passed the most wonderful paintings and architecture, but I have no recollection of any of it. My mind was on our meeting with the Queen, hoping that I wouldn't do or say anything that would be out of place. We were told that she would first greet some newly appointed bishops before making her way to speak to Peter and me.

The time came for us to take our places, and we were led to a point directly in front of the steps the royal party would come down. By now the nine thousand guests had also assembled, with half on one side of the huge lawn and half on the other, leaving an avenue about fourteen feet wide. Peter and I were asked to stand in the middle of this avenue. The Queen couldn't have missed us, even if she had wanted to! The two couples we had come with must have wondered why we were standing there, as must several army officers that I spotted, much higher in rank than Peter!

At last a hush descended over the crowd as the royal

party emerged from the building, and came down the steps. The Queen was accompanied by Prince Philip. Also in the party were Princess Anne and Prince Charles. After the Queen had had a short word with the bishops, she came over to us. Peter glanced at his watch as she approached, wondering how much time we would get to speak to her. She approached Peter with the words, 'I'm so pleased to meet you, Captain Barlow. I've heard a lot about you.' This made me smile, as Peter was only a lieutenant, and I wondered if she knew something that we didn't yet know! She then held out her hand to me, and I grasped it, remembering to bob in a curtsey, grateful that I didn't get my legs all jumbled up!

The Queen asked Peter his opinion on some of the decisions that had been taken during the conflict, occasionally drawing me into the conversation. But for the main, I stood and listened in awe, not quite believing that we were able to spend so much time with the Queen, while the rest of the nine thousand guests waited patiently. Finally she bade us goodbye, and went to talk to the many other people waiting for a glimpse and possibly a word, having spent a total of seventeen minutes chatting to us both. I thought she looked slightly pale and tired, but it was wonderful to meet her. Afterwards we went for a cream tea in one of the big marquees which had been erected in the grounds, before walking around the lake and the magnificent gardens that surround the Palace. For the rest of the day we had people coming up to us, asking why we spent so much time with the Queen, and what she had said. It was certainly a special day that will go down into the Barlow family history.

Peter had been going to a weekly Bible study. The one he linked in with was run by SASRA, the Soldiers and Airmen's Scripture Readers Association, specifically for people who worked in the armed forces. He told me that they were looking round for a new place to meet. I knew that he was hoping I would suggest our house. But I was reluctant because I still felt so out of my depth as far as spiritual things were concerned. In the end, though, I agreed, much to Peter's surprise and delight.

Now it was my turn to feel out of place again. The people were warm and friendly, but I didn't know anyone, and wished I was more knowledgeable about spiritual things. They would take a whole evening discussing one or two Bible verses, really studying every possible shade of meaning, going from one reference point to the next to back up their thoughts. I wanted so much to understand things the way they seemed to, but I felt frustrated because I knew I had to read the Bible on a regular basis if I was to make any sense out of it. The problem was that everyone thought I had far more understanding than I did, and I just didn't know who I could turn to to help me in my dilemma.

Peter came home one day and told me that he had been invited by the army to take a two-year short-term posting to Calgary in Canada. He was obviously keen, but I wasn't, and my two words to him were, 'No thanks.' So the idea was dropped, but came up again about three months later. This time for some reason the idea had more appeal, and once I was satisfied that the children could join us in their school holidays (Andrew had already started boarding school, and Laura started a term before we left for Canada) I agreed – when Peter promised there would be no invasions! Another change was about to take place in our life, but Canada became a side-issue compared to what was just up ahead.

16

Through the Waters

A little while before Canada became an option, in fact before the children had gone to boarding school, I started to attend a Tuesday morning Bible study for ladies, which was run by Barbara Moody, the SASRA leader's wife. I enjoyed taking part in the discussions and hearing more of the Bible explained. During coffee one morning I heard one of the group ask Lynn if she was going to a Bible study group to be held that Thursday evening. Lynn had a little boy called Curtis who suffered badly from cerebral palsy. A few weeks earlier, she had taken Curtis to this group, they had prayed for him, and just a week later he was doing all kinds of things that he had never been able to do before. Lynn nodded enthusiastically, indicating that she was definitely going along. My curiosity was sufficiently aroused to ask if I could go too. It sounded interesting. Lynn was delighted that I wanted to go, and so on Thursday evening I set off, not quite knowing what to expect, leaving Peter at home with the children.

The meeting was held in the home of Jeremy and Daphne, a couple in their sixties, who I sensed really loved the Lord and who had a sound knowledge of the Bible. Jeremy had white hair and was of average height and build. He had a gentle but strong personality, and became someone I found it easy to talk to. Daphne, his wife, had darkish hair, turning grey, and a pleasant personality. She too was easy to talk to, and was very much a cat lover. She had a wonderful gift of hospitality, and made everyone who visited her neat home feel welcome.

I felt an air of expectancy as about a dozen men and women squeezed into their cosy living room, where kitchen chairs had been placed between their normal living-room furniture to give everyone somewhere to sit. The meeting started with choruses, followed by a lively discussion of the Bible, everyone chipping in with their comments or thoughts. Then, before tea and biscuits were served, there was a time of waiting on the Lord, when some people spoke in tongues, something that I hadn't really come across before, while others had interpretations and prophecies, some general and others specific for people at the meeting. It was all very new and exciting for me.

Even though the meeting was made up of people that I didn't know, I felt that I could just be myself, and didn't have to pretend that I was something I wasn't, or that I knew more than I did. At the end of the meeting I made a beeline for Jeremy, and asked him why he thought it was that I was having such a hard time reading and understanding the Bible.

'Tell me how you are going about it,' he asked kindly, as he sipped his cup of tea, at the same time offering me a biscuit, which I accepted gratefully. 'Well,' I said, trying to explain what I had been experiencing as simply as I could, 'I've been reading from Genesis. In fact I've started to read it several times, but each time I seem to get bogged down somewhere in Exodus or Numbers and then give up.'

Jeremy explained that the Bible was not like a normal book, and you didn't have to start at the beginning. 'In fact, it would be much more helpful if you started to read some of the New Testament first – preferably in a modern translation. Then by all means read some of the Old Testament as well. I'm sure that way you will start to understand things a lot better.' This was brilliant advice, and just what I needed to hear. Why oh why hadn't I had the courage to ask someone before?

I went home full of news about the Bible study, and told Peter all that I could remember about the choruses, the informal Bible study, and then the prayer time afterwards. Peter had his doubts about what I told him had gone on. He wasn't sure about the speaking in tongues and the 'words' that were given out. I tried to explain how it had been, but in the end we decided that the only way he could ever know what it was like was if he went himself. So when the next Thursday came, Peter went to the meeting, and I stayed at home with the children, wishing for the first time that it was the other way around, and wondering what he would make of it all. I need not have worried. Peter came home later that evening feeling as positive about the group as I did, and so from then on we had to take turns until the children went to boarding school which released us both to go.

Soon after that, my friend Barbara, the Padre's wife, asked me if I would like to go with her to a Christian Viewpoint meeting in the nearby town of Salisbury. She explained that a luncheon would be served, after which a speaker would give a talk for about twenty minutes or so. The guest speaker was to be Jenny Rees Larcombe, who had been in a wheelchair when she was booked to speak several months before, but in the interim had received a remarkable healing. This reminded me of what had happened to Lynn's little boy, and I eagerly went along.

Jenny gave an interesting and challenging talk about how a personal relationship with Jesus had changed her life, both physically and spiritually, and explained that unless we had a personal encounter with Him and invited Him into our hearts, according to scripture we would not have a place in heaven. She reminded us that Jesus Himself said, 'I am the way, the truth and the life. No one comes to the Father except through me' (John 14:6). This was news to me. No one had told me before that there was something that *I* had to do. Jenny didn't ask anyone to put up their hands or go to the front or anything, but just to pray the prayer that she said, silently in their hearts, as she said it. I bowed my head and prayed, glad at last that I knew I was accepted by God. But doubts soon came in, and when I went to a similar meeting some weeks later, I found myself praying the same prayer, and then again, until I realised that no matter how I felt, God only wanted me to pray that particular prayer once! I had not told anyone what I had done, seeing it as a personal thing between me and God. Because I had gone to church for so long, I had in any case considered myself a Christian. From now on I would describe myself as a *committed* Christian. As I started to read the Bible as Jeremy had suggested, I realised that Jesus had died on the Cross for *me*. Before, if I had thought about it at all, I just took it as an inclusive thing, done for the whole world in general.

A short time later, at the Tuesday morning meeting, as one of the ladies, Angie, was mulling over what we would be studying, she suddenly turned to me and for no apparent reason said, quite forcefully, 'And *you* need to get baptised!' Everyone stared at me and I felt embarrassed and angry. I wondered why she had suddenly come out with this statement, and in such a public way. I tried to make light of it, saying that I had been christened and confirmed already. The moment passed, but to my horror, she did the same thing the very next week! This time, I broke down in tears, wondering why Angie was singling me out, when others in the group had never been baptised or confirmed for all I knew!

In the preceding months I had been reading the Bible daily, fascinated by all it had to say. Now for the first time the Bible was coming alive for me, and I understood how Jesus loved me even with all my faults and failures. He loved me enough to be crucified on a cross and die for me, and He was my very own personal Saviour. He loved me for no other reason than that I'm me! Now I couldn't read the Bible enough, and hungrily digested every word. I asked Jesus to guide my life and my footsteps. It was good to be walking forward in my Christian life. Nearly two years had passed since our escapades in Iraq, and I felt very content with my life. But the comments that Angie had made to me concerning believer's baptism just would not go away.

That week it was my turn to go to the Thursday evening house-group meeting. I shared with Jeremy what had been said to me. Listening carefully as I spilled out my tale, he thought for a moment and after I had finished said, 'Look, Sheila, nobody has the right to tell anyone to get baptised. It's a personal decision that people need to come to as they feel led by the Lord. Tell you what, though, I have a video on the subject that you and Peter can watch, which would give you a little more information.' Soon the video was in my hands, and after watching the tape several times later that week Peter and I felt that this indeed was what God was leading us towards.

My baptism was not a spur of the moment thing. I spent much time deliberating about it, partly because I'm a 'stay in the background and make the tea' sort of person, so the thought of being the centre of attention at a baptismal service was going against my natural pattern of behaviour. This I had to struggle with, but far outweighing that was the fact that I had decided now was the time to stand up and tell others that I loved Jesus. My believer's baptism was a new beginning in my Christian life. Although I knew that faith in Jesus is the one thing that is needed in order to go to heaven, I felt as though I had been changed in some way with a new commitment. I knew with certainty that I believed totally in God and trusted Him to guide my life. So, one Sunday morning a few weeks later, at a little free church that Jeremy had connections with, both Peter and I went through the waters of baptism. Both of us were so glad that we had taken that further step of faith. Angie had been right after all!

17

Strange Voices

One night, a week later, I was lying in bed trying to get to sleep. I felt tired out, but my mind would not turn off. I could hear Peter breathing gently beside me, and I tried to keep as still as possible so as not to wake him. I thought of all that I had to do the next day, and just wished that sleep would overtake my restless mind. Then, as I lay there in the darkness, I became aware of a voice. It wasn't anything in the room, I knew that. It was a voice in my head.

'*Sheila,*' it said in a seductive way, '*Sheila, I have something to tell you.*'

It was talking about a couple who used to go to the Thursday evening group, saying that they needed to repent; if they did they would be forgiven and accepted back into the fellowship, and I needed to tell them this. Could it be that I was having words from the Lord, like some of the people in the Thursday group? I supposed that this was the case. After a while, in spite of the persistence of the voice, which seemed to go on and on, I managed to get off to sleep.

I hesitantly mentioned the incident to Peter the next morning, wondering what he would think, and what I should do. He agreed with me that things like this had to be tested, to see whether they were from the Lord or not. We agreed that the best thing I could do was to ask the advice of Jeremy and Daphne.

They listened in silence as, sitting round their coffee table later that morning, I explained to them what had happened the night before. They nodded occasionally, in acknowledgment of the fact that they understood what I was saying.

'Have you tested what you feel you had from the Lord?' asked Jeremy.

'As much as I can,' I said, not sure of how I would do that. 'I can't see how what I had would be in any way harmful if I shared it with the couple concerned . . .'

Just as we were chatting, another member of the group turned up. Jo was someone who had been having problems in her life, and she came round to see Jeremy and Daphne, as many of the group did. After they had prayed for her for some fears that she was struggling with, she left. I happened to mention that for a long time I had had a fear of the dark, and they suggested that they pray for me. I agreed, but before I knew what was happening, they started to call upon a spirit of fear to come out of me. This wasn't what I had expected, even though I had heard that they had a deliverance ministry. They raised their voices, commanding the demon of fear to be expelled. After a while they stopped, obviously feeling that the work had been done, even though I have to admit that I didn't feel any different. I went home soon afterwards, and drifted off into a fitful sleep on the sofa.

When I woke up a little while later the room seemed eerily silent and I had the strange sensation that something was very wrong. I felt as though I was shut in an empty vacuum, totally alone, as though my communication with God through prayer had been severed, and that He had left me, which made me panic.

I grabbed hold of the phone and with shaking hands dialled Jeremy's number. When he answered I blurted out my fears in a voice that was now a croak and fading fast. My breathing was coming in gulps as I begged him to come over. Jeremy said that he couldn't come over as their policy was that people always visited them for ministry, so that it could never be said that they were forcing themselves on anyone against their wishes. But realising the state I was in he reluctantly relented and said that he would also contact Peter. Before putting the phone down Jeremy tried to reassure me that everything would be fine; God had promised that He would never leave me, and that there was no way anything or anyone could separate me from him. They were comforting words but I still felt very fearful.

Soon Peter's car was pulling up on the driveway and we waited for Jeremy and Daphne to arrive, neither of us quite knowing what to say to each other. Immediately Jeremy and Daphne arrived they started a full-blown deliverance ministry on me. They called on various kinds of demons to come out of me. By this time, I was on the floor, screaming and wriggling around, while Peter looked on, occasionally holding me down, looking and feeling more and more uncomfortable about all that was happening to me in our living room. Eventually I became quieter, the deliverance session was brought to a halt and after a brief chat they left.

I can't say I felt much better than before they arrived. Peter, however, was very angry. He was angry at what had happened, angry with me, angry that he didn't understand what was going on any more. I didn't know what to say in my defence, as I didn't understand either. All I knew was that I felt more and more out of control of my own thoughts and feelings, and that I was causing hurt and anger to those I loved the most. I was glad at least that the children were by this time away at boarding school.

The weekend arrived, and with it a new problem. Some information concerning Canada had arrived for Peter at my parents' house, their address being one we would often give if we weren't sure where we would be at a future date. He needed to collect the information and asked if I would go with him. I said no, the reason being that I wasn't sure how I was going to react any more. I didn't want Peter getting cross with me again, or Mum and Dad seeing me in the state I was in. Peter was puzzled and angry that I didn't want to go to my own parents with him, and said that he was going on his own. I asked if he would take me to Jeremy and Daphne's for the weekend, and he reluctantly agreed, dropping me off on his way to my parents. When Peter had left I sat and talked with them for a while. They came to the conclusion that I needed more prayer, so they called on a friend to come and help them continue what they had started a few days before.

Their friend arrived, and soon I was being asked to name every fear I ever had. I didn't know where to start – or stop! I mentioned a few things, and another deliverance ministry started, with me again rolling round on the floor, screaming and crying. The sadness that I had felt when I had miscarried came to the surface, and I found myself saying that Peter had never wanted the babies, and all sorts of other odd, strange things. I was encouraged to spit the 'demons' into a bucket, and name anything and everything that I thought was relevant. Eventually the session was over and, excusing myself, I departed for some rest.

I was alone again, this time in a little single bed that they had made up for me in their spare room. I felt oh so tired and confused after all the events of the last few hours, but in spite of that my mind would not relax and allow me the rest that I so badly needed. Suddenly, the voice was back with me again.

'*Sheila, are you listening to me? You must keep listening to me. I want you to get out of bed, and straighten the bedclothes.*' That sounded reasonable enough. This was the voice of Jesus talking to me, I was sure. I got out of bed and did what I was told. All I wanted to do was to obey Jesus. I could remember saying that at my baptism, and everyone had been pleased.

'*Sheila,*' the voice said again, '*I want you to get some salt from Jeremy and Daphne. I want you to wash your body, and especially your ears, in salt water. But don't rinse it off.*'

If that was what Jesus wanted me to do, I would do it. No question about that. I hadn't been in bed for long, and I went downstairs and asked Jeremy and Daphne if I could have some salt. Daphne looked a little puzzled, but went into the kitchen and gave me some salt which I took without explanation along the passage and into the bathroom, where I washed as instructed in salt water. I just wanted to obey the voice of Jesus from now on.

After a fitful night's rest, I dressed and went down for breakfast. Daphne had prepared a light meal for me of cereal, toast and a pot of tea. Was it right for me to eat what she had prepared? I waited for instructions.

'*It's OK, Sheila, you can eat what is on the table,*' said the voice. I noticed that Jeremy and Daphne had seen me hesitate before starting to eat, but maybe they just thought I was thanking the Lord for my food. They made no comment, but when Peter arrived to take me home, Jeremy took him to one side and told him that I was acting strangely, and not to get angry with me, as I was obviously confused. Poor Peter, I'm sure he wondered by now just what was happening to his wife.

I felt exhausted by the time I got home, even though

Jeremy and Daphne lived only a short way away. I went upstairs for a rest, as Peter and I were scheduled to go out that evening to the free church where we were baptised, for a Harvest Thanksgiving service. After a couple of hours I got up, but the voice was still there, instructing me on what I should do, what I should wear, what I should say. By now, I didn't think the voice was at all unusual. It was just part of me, or so I thought.

Peter and I went to the service as planned, although neither of us was saying much to each other, both lost in our own thoughts. The service consisted of several little plays put on by various people, interspersed with testimonies and suchlike. I sat there, fascinated – not because of what was going on, but because I knew what was going to happen before it actually did! I would hear the voice say, '*They are going to call on that person to speak next,*' and, sure enough, they did. Then I would be told the next thing that would happen. I still felt very tired and my head ached, but I tried to enter into the mood of the evening.

The voice kept chattering away in my head, giving me no peace. It was no longer informing me of the events unfolding before my eyes, but was giving me information about myself. '*Sheila, I'm very sorry to have to tell you this,*' said the voice, '*but you're a witch. And because you're a witch and Peter is a Christian, he's going to kill you, or you're going to kill him.*'

This was horrible news that the Jesus voice was giving me. But I knew Jesus couldn't be wrong. I must be a very wicked person indeed. What was going to happen to Peter and me? I felt distraught, and burst into tears. Peter looked at me in dismay and asked what was wrong. I said that it was nothing, not wanting to bother him with this terrible news that the Jesus voice had given me. Peter made excuses to those around us, and we left the church with people staring at us, wondering why I was so upset.

Then, as we were driving along in the car, the voice said that Andrew was already dead, and that he had been killed in a road accident. *'He's already in hell, waiting for you,'* it said in a matter-of-fact way. I knew Andrew was travelling that day, so guessed that it was true.

Every so often Peter asked why I was so upset, but I told him nothing. If he knew I was a witch, he would kill me for sure. The voice had told me so and I didn't want him to have to do anything so awful. There was no way I wanted to kill him, so I guessed the only way out of this problem was if I killed myself. I had no other choice. I was devastated. Peter glanced at me and asked if I was feeling any better. 'It will be all right,' I said as I forced a weak smile. 'Everything's going to be OK.'

All I needed to do now was to find the best way of killing myself. I thought of taking the car and crashing it, but reasoned that that might harm someone else. I felt cross with myself that I couldn't think of an effective way of getting rid of myself. I thought of taking an overdose of pills, but was afraid I would be discovered before they could do their work. I was for the first time feeling both depressed and desperate, as I contemplated what I had to do to stop either Peter or me killing each other.

The rest of the journey was made in silence as I struggled with my thoughts. When we arrived home, Peter went into the living room, wanting a few moments by himself to try and stem the frustration and apprehension that was growing in him. Meanwhile, I ran into the kitchen. I grabbed a carving knife, and rushed out of the back door, down the path, and into the wood at the end of the garden. When I didn't join Peter in the living room after a few minutes, he came looking for me, and, when there was no sign of me in the house, he guessed that I had gone to a friend's house. He rang one or two people he thought I might have gone to, but when they sounded surprised that he didn't know where I was, decided not to ring anyone else, as by now it was getting quite late. Instead he decided to wait up for me, and went back into the living room.

By this time, I had stumbled into the wood, certain in my mind that I was still obeying the Jesus voice. I got the knife, and plunged it into my chest, and then fell on it, to make sure that it did its job. I fully intended to kill myself, in order to obey the voice within me. In my normal state of mind I hated even the sight of blood, and needles terrified me, but in my normal state of mind I would never have thought that Jesus would have put me through such an ordeal. Although I didn't know it then, I was very ill, alone and bleeding to death in a wood, and nobody knew what I had done or where I was.

As I lay there I became aware of another voice. This was a mocking voice which I identified as the Devil's voice. As with the Jesus voice, it grabbed my attention by starting the sentence with my name, and then went on to use words and phrases that I didn't think I knew, and certainly didn't use, which wrongly confirmed in my own mind that these were voices of other beings.

This new voice said, '*Sheila, why don't you ask Jesus to save you? He could do, you know.*'

I shouted out, 'No, no!' I knew that the only way out was for me to die. I didn't want to kill anyone or be murdered. I *had* to take my own life.

'*But Sheila, you can live,*' the Satan voice continued. '*you can serve me in a psychiatric hospital for the rest of your life.*'

I listened, horrified at what was being suggested. There

was no way that I wanted to serve the Devil, in a psychiatric hospital or anywhere else.

Time went on, with the full moon casting eerie shadows around me. I was in great pain, with the Satan voice taunting me that if I thought I was in pain now, just wait until I died and went to hell! As I lay on the ground, occasionally hearing the wildlife in the woods shuffling around, I tried to concentrate on what the Jesus voice was saying and block out the Satan voice. With great effort I pulled the knife out of my chest, hoping this would speed things up, which caused me even more pain. I had lost quite a lot of blood, and felt at times as if I was floating, unsure of which noises were real or imaginary. I had been lying on the root of a small tree, which added to the pain I was already experiencing from my knife wound. The Devil's voice taunted me that many of my family were dead, and this was to be my fate very soon.

I lay for many hours, drifting in and out of consciousness. Then, as daylight began to disperse the darkness and the moon was low on the horizon, I heard a gentle voice speaking to me.

'*Sheila, you may go home now.*'

'How can that be?' I questioned.

'*Go home to Peter,*' the voice continued, '*and ask him to take you to hospital. The witch inside you is no more.*'

18

Safe – and Secure

I stumbled back to the house, holding myself so I didn't
lose any more blood, leaving the knife behind in the woods.
Peter had spent the night dozing on the sofa, thinking that I
was with a friend and would come home when I had calmed
down, so nothing could have prepared him for what he now
saw, as I stood in the kitchen, pleading with him to get
me to a hospital. Fortunately for me, as always his army
training kicked into action, and he gently helped me into
the car and drove me to the local hospital, saying very little
as we drove there. As it turned out, the first hospital he
chose did not have a casualty department, so we drove to
another one, where they stitched me up as best they could.
Fortunately I did not know enough about my anatomy to
inflict the kind of damage that I wanted to. And I shall be
always grateful for the fact that the thought never entered
my head to slash my wrists. There would have been no
second chances had I taken that course of action.

The doctor and nurses wanted to know precisely what
had happened to me, and why I had done what I had done.
I told them quite simply everything that I had been told by
the voices, and when the medical staff asked if I thought
I was likely to do it again I said, 'No.' Jesus had told me
there was no need any more. But I had a new problem.

The Jesus voice told me that I was pregnant, and that Peter was trying to kill the baby. I screamed out my fears. Peter tried to talk to me calmly, but I was having none of it. After monitoring my heart, X-rays and an ultrasound were taken before I was placed on a drip and taken to an observation ward. Peter was encouraged by the hospital staff to go home and get some rest.

The ward which I was put in contained just a few people who were obviously very ill. The voices soon started to give me 'information' concerning the *real* reason that I was there.

'*Sheila, they're going to try and kill you,*' they said. '*Watch out, and be on your guard.*'

I was suspicious of everyone, and decided that what I was being offered to eat and drink had been tampered with. I refused to eat or drink anything, but then, I hadn't eaten anything for several days before my attempt on my life anyway. I refused medication, as I guessed that was probably poisoned too, and I didn't want to harm the baby I was carrying. Eventually they gave me a pregnancy test to prove that I was not pregnant, which confused me further. I didn't know who I could trust. The nurses were kind, but sometimes the glint I saw in their eyes, brought on no doubt by tiredness, was enough to awaken my suspicions.

The voices were still as insistent as ever, telling me that close friends had died in car crashes, and that Peter had also died, which was soon disproved when he walked through the doors to visit me! Rest was a luxury that evaded me. One day I attempted to walk out of the hospital, as the Jesus voice had assured me that Peter was waiting for me outside the building. Two nurses took my arms and encouraged me to return to the ward. On another occasion I walked up and down the wards singing hymns at the top of my voice in the belief this would protect me from evil.

Then I came into contact with John. He was a fresh-faced young nurse, who seemed happy and relaxed. I asked him if he was a Christian, and when he answered that his parents occasionally went to church and he sometimes had accompanied them, that was enough for me! Here was someone I could put my confidence in! From then on, I would trust him with anything. I looked upon him as my guardian angel.

Eventually the hospital staff finished their analysis of me, and decided that I needed psychiatric help. I was told by one of the health visitors, a lovely lady called Pat, what type of hospital I would be taken to, and what I could expect. What she did not realise was that they weren't going to put me in an 'open' hospital, but in a very secure unit. Peter signed the necessary forms for me to be admitted there, and an ambulance came to take me on my journey. I was accompanied not by Pat, but by her assistant, a nice enough woman but lacking Pat's warmth and care. At the end of the short journey I was carried out of the ambulance on a stretcher. As I passed through the various sections of the hospital on the way to the ward, metal doors would be unlocked, and then banged firmly behind me. This hospital appeared to resemble a prison rather than a place of healing.

As I was pushed along the corridor my ears picked up the disturbed screams of someone in deep distress. I discovered later that they came from an adolescent who had been put in a padded room, and he was screaming for his mother. There were other horrible, unfamiliar noises and sights as I made my progress through this hospital which was to be my secure place for the foreseeable future. I was eventually put into a tiny room with gloomy grey walls and a metal-framed bed. The woman who had accompanied me from the general hospital soon made her excuses and left, closing the door after her, leaving me completely alone.

As I lay there on the bed my eyes flew to the closed door. One of the problems I was battling with was claustrophobia, so to be shut in such a confined space made me feel panicky. Just as I was about to scream for help the door reopened and a young nurse walked into my 'cell' and proceeded to read me my rights under the Mental Health Act. In fact what she read firmly stated that I had no rights! She said that I was to be detained for one month, after which time I would be reassessed. The only other way I could leave this unit would be with written permission from a court of law. She also stated that I had no right to refuse medication or food, otherwise it would be forced upon me. Her duty performed, she walked through the door, leaving me again utterly alone.

Mentally ill. The thought hit me for the first time like a bolt from the blue. I was mentally ill! I slumped further down under the covers of my bed, stunned that I could be in such a state in such a place. How could this be? This couldn't be happening to me, could it? I stared at the ceiling, my vision blurred by my tears, trying to make some kind of sense out of a senseless situation. I remembered everything that I had done, and because the voices were still going on in my brain, I felt very afraid. For all I knew this was going to be my new *permanent* home. Didn't that Satan voice say in the woods that I could serve him for ever if I was willing to live in a psychiatric hospital? But it was not my choice that I was here, and I certainly didn't want to serve him anywhere – only Jesus.

Everything was crowding in on me. I just wanted to curl up in a corner and let the world go by. I was frightened, completely and utterly defeated, with no hope left in sight. Words could never explain just how wretched I was feeling.

How could this happen when I had committed myself such a short time ago to Jesus? Wasn't life supposed to get easier – not tougher? I was at rock bottom and it was not a pleasant place to be. I was hurting . . . big time!

The next few days were very difficult and I found it hard to relate to anyone, but then I gradually started to come round again. There was no more fight left in me. I couldn't refuse food or drink any more, and I was finally convinced by the staff that they weren't trying to kill me, and that I wasn't pregnant. I still suffered pain from the wound that I had inflicted upon myself, and continued to feel constantly tired. One thing that I did hate was the door being closed on me. Every time a nurse shut it, I waited a few moments and then I would get up and open it again. After a while, when they realised that I wasn't going to go anywhere, they let me keep it open, just a little bit, which was enough to make me feel more relaxed.

For the first three days I was watched constantly, even when taking a bath, in my allocated two inches of cold water! After three days, they must have decided that I was well enough to be allowed to go to the toilet on my own, which I suppose was some kind of privilege! The toilet door had no lock to secure it and I struggled to close it because of the pain in my chest. Turning round I froze to the spot. Lying on the floor was a green army belt. There were only nine people in the hospital, but by a bizarre coincidence one of the patients was a lad of about twenty who had a fetish about army uniform! The army belt was his. The belt on the floor brought back the terror I had felt when I was in the bathroom in Kuwait, and I had seen those brown masculine arms reaching out to try and get me. The belt made me break into a cold sweat, and I screamed and refused to use the toilet. This and other incidents that happened confirmed to the doctors that I was suffering from post-traumatic stress disorder.

The staff asked the lad, whose name was Mike, not to wear his uniform; he reluctantly agreed, but for some unknown reason he continued to wear his belt, which caused me to cower away from him whenever he came near. He was probably young enough to be my son, with fairly long hair, an abrupt way of speaking, and a very serious disposition. Looking back, there was no real reason to fear him, but at the time everything seemed real enough.

I started to pray, remembering how it had helped me in the past. But now it was different. When I now tried to pray to God, and tell Him what was happening to me and how I was feeling, the Jesus voice or the Satan voice would answer me, and I would become terribly confused. I tried so very hard to be strong and think sensibly, but all to no avail. I realised that as I forced myself to pray, things were getting worse; the voices would taunt me until I lost all sense of reality. I prayed constantly, which only stressed me more. I was as weak and helpless as a babe in arms.

It was at this point I accepted I could do no more, it was beyond me, and I did what I should have done a long time before. I let go of my self-dependency and totally put my trust in God. I had to do this by faith and just trust and wait. I prayed one last prayer to God:

Dear Heavenly Father,
I am so sorry I have failed you. I don't know what else I can do. I can't even pray to you any more. I give up trying, and place myself into your hands. Please forgive me that I can no longer talk to you.
Amen.

As I finished my simple prayer, the scripture verse 'Be still and know that I am God' came into my mind, and I hung on to that verse. It's a short verse, but brought me great comfort. It said it all. The most active thing I could do was to be still and stop fighting. I wanted to know where I could find the verse in the Bible, but I couldn't find a Bible anywhere. In any case the medication made it impossible for me to read even a few lines of anything, and my concentration was all but gone.

19

Recovery and Reflection

After the first couple of days I was expected to eat with the other patients in the dining room, which at first I found difficult, partly because of the voices that were constantly chattering away in my brain, partly because this made it hard to avoid Mike and his army belt, and partly because I just wanted to be left alone. Peter visited me every day, always wearing his best suit and trying to be as positive as he could. Maybe his choice of attire was his way of saying that he was still in control and able to look after himself, I don't really know.

Conversation with him was difficult as the voices inside my head kept giving me orders. He would say something, and one of the voices would say, *'Tell him this,'* and then say what I needed to convey to him. So there were long pauses in the conversation while I listened to Peter and then to the instructions that I was getting. It was most confusing for me, and no doubt for poor Peter too. He told me later that he thought at this point he had lost me for ever, as he had never seen anyone like that before.

The other problem was that Peter felt he really had no one to talk to. If anyone else had a problem they would go to him, as Family Officer, and he would try and sort it out. But who does the Family Officer go to in an emergency?

I'm sure there would have been other officers and friends he could have turned to, but whether out of pride or embarrassment or whatever he didn't. In the end when my hospital phoned the army to check something out, the truth was revealed, which gave him no choice but to share with his contemporaries the problems that he was facing.

After that I started to get some visitors other than Peter, which was nice but very tiring. I tried to act normally but knew that I wasn't making a very good job of it. My visitors had not realised what kind of hospital I was in, so the first expression on their faces would be one of shock and horror before they regained their composure. I was by now well enough to feel embarrassed at my own predicament, which brought me a new illness – wounded pride.

One of my visitors was Jean, who had shared so many of my experiences in the Gulf. I felt ashamed at her seeing me in this hospital, especially as in the past I had spoken to her about my faith in God. What I didn't know at the time was that she was thinking that it could very well have been her in the next room, as she had been very near to going over the edge herself. A little while after her visit I got a card from Jean and her family with a note saying 'I'm praying for you.' This jumped out at me as I didn't know they had any church connections; I found out later that before going to Kuwait Jean had attended church, but had let it lapse as her husband did not go along with her, thus avoiding family divisions. Since that time things had changed. They had both attended the church service Peter had requested in Iraq, and during Sean's captivity he spent time contemplating his faith, or lack of it. Jean had also been re-examining her own beliefs. So a lot of things had made an impression on both Sean and Jean, and they had each made a fresh commitment to God and were now strong members of their local fellowship. Unbeknown to me, Jean was now part of a prayer group who were praying for me.

I had visitors most days. Derek and Barbara were the new SASRA readers in our area. They would visit me together, hold my hand and pray for me. I really appreciated their visits and their kindness. The Colonel's wife was another visitor. She was kind, but I suspect came partly to assess for herself whether I was in a fit state to go to Canada on our posting, which was just a month away.

It was while I was in this hospital that I had a visit from Jeremy and Daphne, whose prayers for me seemed to trigger the events that found me in this place. They were concerned about my condition of course, but I felt no anger or bitterness towards them, as I knew that they had been genuinely trying to help me, and that the extreme tension that I had been subjected to during the time of the invasion and since had far more to do with the way things had turned out than their ministry had done. They visited again when I was discharged, and we have remained friends.

The days in the hospital started to take on their own strange routine. In the morning we all had to meet at a certain time to discuss what needs we had, like toiletries, chocolate or suchlike. I kept asking for a newspaper, but each time I did they would make a different excuse – the shop had sold out, or they had forgotten to get one, or they had had none delivered. They made me feel like a complete nonentity which left me very frustrated. I wanted a newspaper of my own! A newspaper was in fact delivered to the ward every day, but it was always being used by someone, or the nurses would take it away and pass it among themselves, and it never returned. I could only manage to read for a few minutes before my sight or concentration let me down, and needed my own paper so I could pick it up and read it little and often as a discipline.

I was afraid that otherwise the little concentration I still had would vanish.

Eventually one of the nurses, who was married to a soldier in the army, struck up a conversation with me. She was stunned to find out that I was an officer's wife, as I certainly didn't conform to the normal image. The link that we both had with the army caused a bond between us, and she used to smuggle a newspaper into the hospital each day for me to read.

Time passed very slowly. The days seemed long and drawn out, and I had plenty of time to dwell on my predicament. Each day I was being assessed by the hospital staff as they tried to determine what progress I was making. I was asked by one of the student nurses to write down all my thoughts, everything that was going through my mind. This was hard for me. The medication made my eyesight hazy, my concentration was like a one-year-old's, and my thoughts were jumbled, to say the least. However, I did manage to write something down on paper, only to cross much of it out at a later date because I didn't like what I had written, much to the annoyance of the nurse!

I began to realise that I was getting used to my new surroundings and seeing them as a secure and safe place, where all the pressures and tensions of the world couldn't get to me. Everything was provided, and I was asked to do only what the staff thought I was capable of. Maybe life wasn't too bad here after all. I was even getting used to the screams and disturbances that were common every day. But just as I was nearing the point of wanting to stay in this nice safe haven for ever, things began to change. I was becoming more aware of what was going on around me.

One of the women in the hospital with me was called Helen. Helen was anorexic, and as a result was very thin. With straight, wispy fair hair, which either fell over her face or was scraped back over her head, she was quite a disturbed character. Although I wanted to talk to her, I found her difficult to relate to, partly because of her unpredictability. Part of her problem was that she sought the attention of others any way she could. She would often try and steal drugs from the trolley, or throw cups of tea across the room, smashing them on the wall with a crash. Now that I was relating to what was happening around me I felt as if I was one of the staff; therefore, if I was the only other person in the room at the time of these events I would try and stop them. This was fine until she started picking up chairs to smash through the window. I grabbed her and yelled for help. When the nurses came running they had to restrain Helen with a lot of force to calm her down. I hated to see her lying on the floor with her arm twisted up her back by two male nurses. This I am sure is how the nurses had been trained, and was probably the normal procedure in such events, but this did not make it any more palatable to me. Helen would scream in agony, and I, along with Stella, the only other female patient, would weep at the sight.

I was becoming uneasy at the things that were occurring. It saddened me to think these patients might always have to live their lives in care. But it took another event to make me want to return to the outside world.

This was when David arrived on the scene. He was a man who had been living on the streets. He was filthy dirty with long hair and a scruffy untended beard. All his clothes had to be taken from him and boiled. Afterwards, poor chap, he went around with sleeves and trouser-legs halfway up his limbs. He was a nice guy really, and I enjoyed talking to him – until I discovered that he had lice! It was not his fault, but I was told they could not treat all the patients as some would react badly and maybe become violent. This was the spur I needed. I thought that maybe this hospital was not where I wanted to be for the rest of my life. I really *did* need to get out of here!

I gradually came to realise that if I was ever to get out of this awful place I needed to try and ignore the voices as best as I could, in the hope that they would go away. That was hard, because they were so insistent, but I knew I had to try. Mike, the lad who was always wearing the army belt, came up to me after I had been there about a fortnight and asked why I was afraid of him. 'I understand that you were caught up in a war somewhere,' he probed. It took all the stamina I possessed not to flee from him. I knew part of my healing would be to face my fears. I briefly explained what I had been through, and why army uniform had such a negative effect on me, and he suddenly said, 'Don't worry, Sheila. From now on, I'll protect you.' After saying this he sauntered away, and I was relieved when I realised that this was one fear that had gone for ever.

Slowly things began to improve for me. In some strange way I was beginning to feel more peaceful than I had for a long time. I still had a lot of fears to overcome, but one by one they were receding. The voices slowly but surely began to be more distant. I had accepted that the Satan voice was false, and a short time later the Jesus voice was also unreal. This did not make them automatically go away, but because I no longer treated them as real, but more as an irritation, I was increasingly able to distance myself from them. I was very aware that the most important thing was to stay as calm as possible, and gradually they became more of an annoying whisper. I continued to cling to the scripture verse 'Be still and know that I am God' – it was the only one I could remember. It soothed my troubled mind and made me aware that God was in control.

After I had been in this secure hospital for about three

weeks, and following a talk with my doctor, I was permitted to go home for the weekend. Peter still had it in his heart to go to Canada, and if that was the case I needed to be around to see what things were to be taken, and what left in storage. The weekend was tiring but seemed to go well, and shortly after that I was discharged from the secure hospital, and taken to the open hospital the health visitor had originally told me I would be going to. I was only there for about a week, and then after reassuring my doctor I was well enough to take responsibility for myself once more, I was allowed to go back to my home and resume my life again.

When I hit rock bottom in the hospital and felt so terribly alone, I asked God to take control, and He did. Within a short while of returning home I picked up our Good News Bible and searched for the scripture verse that I had clung on to. Much to my dismay and puzzlement it was nowhere to be found. It was only after glancing through a friend's New International Bible some months later that I found the verse 'Be still and know that I am God' in Psalm 46:10. How I knew the verse I held on to in the hospital I will never really know, but I like to think this was God's way of reaching out to me in my troubles.

On a wall in our home we have the poem 'Footprints' written by Margaret Fishback Powers. This is what it says:

One night I dreamed a dream.
I was walking along the beach with my Lord.
Across the dark sky flashed scenes from my life.
For each scene, I noticed two sets of footprints
    in the sand,
One belonging to me and one to my Lord.
When the last scene of my life shot before me

I looked back at the footprints in the sand
And to my surprise
I noticed that many times along the path of life
There was only one set of footprints.
I realised that this was at the lowest and saddest
*   times of my life.*
This always bothered me
And I questioned the Lord about my dilemma.
'Lord, you told me when I decided to follow You,
You would walk and talk with me all the way.
But I'm aware that during the most troublesome
*   times of my life*
There is only one set of footprints.
I just don't understand why, when I needed You most
You left me.'
He whispered, 'My precious child,
I love you and will never leave you,
Never ever, during your trials and testings.
When you saw only one set of footprints
It was then that I carried you.'

I have always liked the gentle encouraging words of this poem. Reading them afresh after my spell in hospital they now had special meaning. I can relate so well to what they say. I believe that God really did carry me through my deepest despair and helplessness until I was strong enough to stand. Only then did He ever so gently put me down and encourage me to walk one step at a time. I know that even when we cannot see the hand of God or feel his presence He is always with us. This is His promise to us. Isaiah 41:10 says, 'So do not fear, for I am with you; do not be dismayed, for I am your God. I will strengthen you and help you; I will uphold you with my righteous right hand.'

In a very special way the poem seemed to sum up the state that I had been in and confirm that, through it all, Jesus had been with me. I began to realise that many people know very little about mental illness. It still has a terrible stigma, which is projected on to the sufferer by themselves and by those around them. It is a taboo subject that not many people will willingly talk about. But, as in any illness, you need others to show you kindness, compassion and love, not fear, strange looks and whispers! It can happen to anyone, and it has taken me a long time to realise that it is not something to be ashamed of. After all, it is an *illness*, just like any other kind. It just happens that this particular sickness affects the mind – and the pride – rather than the body.

Looking back, I realise that in the state of mind I was in at the time, I could have succeeded with my intent to end my life. Nothing anyone could have said or done would have stopped me. My family would have been devastated and tried to reason why I had done such a thing, but there would have been no answer to be found. Sometimes the relatives of loved ones blame themselves, and say or think, 'If only we had said this, or done that,' but I know from experience that it is wrong of them to torture themselves with such misplaced guilt, as there was probably little if anything that their actions would have significantly changed. People in those circumstances need to let go of the past and press on with their future, however tough that might be.

I had been through a period of great stress and tension, which had resulted in a nervous breakdown. But God had been through it with me, and a new chapter was opening up in my life. Peter still wanted to go to Canada, and I wanted to go with him.

20

Canadian Interlude

Going to Canada was important for me for at least two reasons. My mental illness had left me with very little self-confidence, and I wanted to make a new start somewhere completely different. I also felt that Peter had lost confidence in my ability just to be normal, and I wanted him to be able to forget what had gone on, and be able to relax with me again without wondering all the time what I might do or say next. But I also knew that Canada was a long way away from the help and support of our friends, as well as the professional help that I had been given. And now that Laura was at boarding school as well as Andrew, it meant that we would only see our children at holiday times. I knew that Peter dearly wanted to take up this exchange visit he had been offered, and that if I didn't go, he couldn't go either. But as we left England with most of our possessions due to follow us a little while later, Canada was actually the last place that I wanted to be heading for.

We flew to Ottawa first of all, where Peter had to sign lots of forms to do with the exchange. When that was over we hit the shops, and were all soon busily trying on big heavy overcoats and snow boots – essential equipment if we were to survive the sub-zero temperatures of the Canadian winter. Then we boarded another plane, which took us to Calgary, where Peter would be based.

We flew into Calgary Airport just behind the first snows of the winter. The whole area was blanketed in white – and it was *cold*. That was my first impression of the land we would live in for the next two years. As it was the Christmas school holidays we had the children with us. They were far more enthusiastic about the snowy scene than I was. We were met by Wayne, the man Peter was to exchange with, and after a short wait for our luggage to come through, we got into his car, ready to catch our first real glimpse of Canada. Soon we were driving past the elaborate Christmas lights which decorated both the outside of the houses and the trees in the gardens. Multi-coloured bulbs twinkled in the darkness, their light reflected by the crisp white snow. There were more gasps of delight from us all as we also spied snowmen with lights glowing inside them, and giant plastic reindeer with shiny red noses. It made the decorations we would normally have in the UK look rather unadventurous.

When we arrived at the house that was to be our home during our stay in Canada we discovered that we had been allocated what was in effect a little house on the prairie! It stood in splendid isolation, with not so much as a fence around it. It didn't even have a garden, as the growing season is so short, with so little being able to grow anyway, that people had long since stopped even bothering to try. Our new home was a three-bedroomed wooden construction, with two of the bedrooms upstairs and the third on the ground floor. Like most houses in that part of the world it also had a basement, which many Canadians make into a family room, but in our case housed the washing machine and freezer.

The day after we arrived, with only our suitcases to

unpack, Peter decided that purchasing a car was the top priority, as it would be impossible to get around without our own transport. We arrived at a used car lot, in our hired car. After looking over one or two vehicles, Peter finally plumped for a big navy-blue American Dodge which seemed in reasonable condition, for a very reasonable asking price. It would only become obvious the next day why this was so. We drove around for a little while before returning home to carry on with settling in.

However, when Peter tried to start the car the next morning, after a night of sub-zero temperatures, it refused to do anything. When we started to phone round to find out if anyone could help, Peter was asked, 'Did you plug the car in last night?' When he answered that he had no idea what they were talking about, it was explained to him that because of the very low night temperatures experienced in Canada, every car has to have a block heater placed under the bonnet, which in turn has to be plugged into the mains electricity supply in order to stop the car from freezing solid. 'If you look under the bonnet you will see where the heater has to go,' he was told. Peter looked, but our car had no such device. No wonder we got it for such a good price! He eventually got it towed back to the garage, where, after a bit of negotiating from Peter, they agreed to fit the necessary device for a small fee. We were learning fast that although the inhabitants of our new country spoke the same language as Britain the country itself was different in quite a few respects.

Christmas Eve arrived – and so did our belongings! Most of the day was spent unpacking all the things we had crated up back in England, and by the end of the day we had completed our task, as well as putting up our Christmas decorations, and were eagerly looking forward to Christmas Day itself.

We had decided to go to the garrison church for their
Christmas Day service, so after opening a few presents
and a hurried breakfast, we unplugged the car and set
off. Sadly, we didn't feel at home or welcome there. It
might have been because, being Christmas, some people
were away, or there were more visitors than normal, but
for whatever reason we sat through the service and then left
the church without anyone talking to us. It didn't bother us
too much, as we had a big turkey cooking in the kitchen of
our little house, with more presents to open, and family and
friends to phone back home later in the day. As it happened
all the lines to Britain were busy on Christmas Day itself,
which was sad, as apart from sending our greetings to our
loved ones back home we wanted to tell them that we were
having a white Christmas, just like the one Bing Crosby
dreamed of!

The next day after lunch we set off on a walk, well
muffled against the cold in our new snow boots and warm
coats. Although the sky was intensely blue and the sun was
shining, the air was bitterly cold. All we had done for the
last two days was overeat, and, cold or not, we needed
some exercise. Peter and I were discussing the church we
had visited the day before when suddenly Andrew said,
'Look, there's a church over there!' Sure enough, just a
short distance away was a church building. We were too
far away and separated by a major road to see anything but
the name written high on the building – Lakeview Baptist
Church.

Peter turned to me and said, 'How about it? Shall we
give this church a visit to see what it's like?'

'Why not?' I replied. 'Maybe this will suit us better.'

Sunday came. We made a calculated guess that the service
would probably start around 11.00 a.m., and got it right. As
we were parking the car we saw people already beginning to

file into the lobby where they took off their big outdoor coats before going into the centrally heated sanctuary. As we were struggling out of our coats, a young girl in her early twenties came up to us.

'Hi, my name's Kim,' she said, offering a hand of greeting. 'Have you visited here before?'

'No, it's our first visit,' I answered.

'Did you have a good Christmas?' she chatted happily as though she was an old friend. After she had walked away Peter whispered to me, 'Well, that's a hundred per cent improvement on the other church already!' I smiled in agreement, wondering what the service would be like.

I soon found that it was less formal in some ways than the Anglican service I had been used to – the hymns were slightly livelier and the sermon was quite a bit longer, about forty minutes as opposed to the Anglican ten minutes. At the end of the service, a lady in her late seventies, whose name was Mary and who was to become a great friend of ours, turned round and as soon as she heard us speak said, 'Oh, you're English! My mum was English. Oh, I love the English people! It's so good to have you here.'

When the service finished, there was someone on the door to shake our hands, and we chatted with yet more people as we put on our winter coats and snow boots again. But the warmth that we now felt was not just coming from our clothes. We both felt welcomed and accepted, and soon decided that this was the church that was right for us. And after a few services, I got used to, and enjoyed, the longer sermons!

The church had several house groups mid-week, and we joined one which met in the home of Allan and Doris. They were a warm friendly couple who were to become close friends during our time in North America. They had a ministry of hospitality, and their cosy home always seemed to be filled with either their friends or the friends of their teenage children.

All too soon the Christmas holiday period was over. We had all had a wonderful time but now the children had to return to boarding school in England. They were in tears as we waved them off at the airport, and it tugged at my heart to let them go. They were, after all, only ten and twelve, but both Peter and I felt it would be better for them to have a good education in Britain than to try and struggle with a different system in Canada, only to return to England in two years' time with exams on the horizon. Sitting in the car on the return journey wiping a tear away I couldn't help wondering if this decision was the correct one. Already I was longing for the Easter holidays to come, and my children had only been gone an hour!

As soon as Christmas was over I registered myself with a doctor, and told her everything that I had been through. She was very sympathetic, and told me that I could contact her whenever I wanted, also suggesting that she would put me in touch with a psychiatrist should that be necessary. When I left Britain I had been given enough medication for a month, and when that ran out I did not apply for any more. I felt that I could manage without it, and events proved me correct. I did find however that the upset of saying goodbye to the children troubled me a little, and the voices returned, not as forcefully as before, but enough to unsettle me. I prayed that things would not escalate, and thankfully they soon departed again.

Canada was the ideal place for me at this time. It was a fresh start. No one knew what I had been through, so I could relax and just get on with my life as normally as possible. I was shy and I suppose a little withdrawn when I arrived, but as time went by my confidence was gradually building up, and I began to enjoy the country and the new friends that we were making. I strongly believe that God knows our needs, and at this time the thing I was needing most was support and friendship, which He provided in abundance. To look for God's handiwork only in the spectacular means you miss out on His provision for you each and every day. I thank God for the treasured friendships that mean so much to me.

Peter too was enjoying his exchange visit. He was in fact the only British officer in Lord Strathcona's Canadian Regiment at that time, and seemed to settle in well with very little effort. We loved the Canadian way of life, with their higher standard of living, which among other things allowed us to eat out several times a week, often with friends. Wednesdays was a 'Two for One' steak night at a local restaurant. Peter and I hardly missed a week, no wonder my bathroom scales groaned every time I stood on them! Life was once more drifting along in a very pleasant way.

We had been living in Canada for nine months when a rumour started circulating that Peter's Canadian regiment were to serve a period of six months in Bosnia. I couldn't believe it at first – this exchange was supposed to be a perk for both of us, and whichever way you looked at it, Bosnia was no perk! Peter could have kicked up a fuss and voiced that he didn't want to go, but Peter, being Peter, readily agreed! For him it was an exciting adventure that he wanted to be part of. I didn't want to stop him, but at the same time I wondered to myself what reaction I might have if I started to worry about him while he was away. I gave my poor husband a bit of an ear-bashing for some weeks as I came to terms with him returning to a war zone and the dangers that held for him, but finally accepted that this was something he felt he just had to do, and therefore I gave him my blessing.

In the summer holidays the children had nine weeks to spend with us. We made the most of this time and went on the most spectacular vacation, driving down through America to Disneyland in California. We had a great time, and it turned out to be a holiday that none of us will ever forget. On the day we returned Peter was told that the rumour had become fact. He would indeed be going to Bosnia in six months' time.

Peter and I had become very involved with our church. The Bible studies were informative and a joy to attend. I found myself growing more positive in joining in discussions and began to pray out loud, confident that I was not being judged on how articulate my words were, or rather weren't! I appreciated the friendship that I had with Doris, whose house group we attended. She had become a friend I spent quite a lot of time with, often shopping and lunching together. Occasionally we would attend a Christian meeting, or just enjoy a chat over a cup of tea. Doris and I are very different in many ways. She is quite tall, while I am short. Doris can always be found wearing nice jewellery and make-up, while I prefer no make-up and casual clothing. Even our musical tastes differ – she enjoys classical pieces while I prefer something a little less serious. Yet for all our differences we enjoyed a strong friendship.

So it came as a shock to hear from another friend one day that Doris was unwell with some kind of mystery illness. Apparently she had lost her vision, was suffering with high blood pressure, and had collapsed. I was told that the doctors were carrying out tests, but they didn't know what was causing Doris's symptoms. She was feeling really drained from the medicine she had been prescribed, and didn't want visitors. I was devastated. My immediate unspoken thought was that it might be a brain tumour. I phoned, but poor Doris was so tired she could only talk for a short time.

After a few days I went round to see her, not knowing what to say. Seeing her anxiety, I shared a little about the problems that I had had after Kuwait, just to let her know that I understood something of what she was going through. This was hard for me to do, as she was the first non-medical person that I had talked to concerning my problems since coming to Canada nearly a year before. In turn, she did her best to reassure me that she would be OK. Doris has a Christian faith that shines through everything she does, and at this time it certainly gave her the courage not to cave in, although quite naturally she wondered what was happening to her.

Why was God allowing this to happen to my friend who showed such kindness to others, I wondered. My heart was heavy as I made my way home. On my return I prayed earnestly, regretting that I had not prayed for Doris while I was with her. I continued to pray for Doris throughout the days that followed, as did many others. I was so troubled about her that it was causing me slight concern about my own health. I came to the conclusion that this was another of those times when I had to let go and let God take over. So I prayed one night that God would do something not just for Doris, but for me also. I was not prepared for the outcome that followed.

Doris rang me the next morning, excitement in every word she spoke. 'I have just received a report from my doctor. I have cataracts,' she continued cheerfully. 'Can you believe that a simple operation will put everything right!' The high blood pressure and the other symptoms, she explained, were apparently caused by anxiety. I chatted to Doris for a little while longer, not really believing this could be true. I am sure Doris must have wondered why

I was so calm instead of elated. After the phone call ended I sat for a while in stunned disbelief. The Lord had sorted out my friend's problem in a most unexpected way.

A few months earlier, when Peter was on a training exercise in California, preparing for his tour of Bosnia, I had attended a service which was much the same as usual, the only difference being that on this particular Sunday a choir from Briarcrest Bible College were to perform a musical item or two. I leaned against the pew and settled down to listen. The music was lovely, the young eager voices filling the church with their melodious tones. The winter sunshine that was coming through the side window was creeping around to the front of the church.

All of a sudden, with a start, I became aware of the words this group was singing. They sang about being a wounded soldier, and the way that God loves us whether we win or are defeated. As they sang, my thoughts went back to my baptism service when I talked about being in the Lord's Army, and my desire to serve Him. The words continued to strike a chord in me as they spoke of Jesus being the protector and the light in the darkness. They also said, 'I am the One you can cry yourself to, my eyes have shared your tears. Whenever you need me, I'll be there. I will be your shield.'

This song so touched me that I leant forward in my pew, put my head down and prayed at the same time as tears were streaming down my face. This I had never done, before or since. I knew that I had stigmatised myself, and that I felt defeated and guilty because of my past, especially having tried to take my own life. I felt as if a guilty secret hung over me and that God wanted to show me that He was my help in every situation, that I had another step to take before I could be free from guilt. That step was to seek help to get beyond where I was at this stage.

I rang the pastor, and told him that I would like to come and see him about something that was on my mind. He agreed to see me on Tuesday morning. Knowing that Doris didn't work on a Tuesday morning, I rang her and asked if she would come with me, which she agreed to do. My pastor, Gordon Sorensen, who was also Doris's brother-in-law, was a man in his late forties, fairly slim and of medium height. As he greeted us he smiled and ushered us into his small book-lined office. He gestured with his hand for us to sit down, Doris choosing the chair by the door, while I took the one in front of the desk. The window to the right let in some natural light, but an electric lamp was needed to give more brightness to the scene. Gordon sat across from me, trying to put me at ease with some general small talk, his hands fidgeting with a ballpoint pen as he spoke.

I found it difficult at first to open up the conversation on why I had wanted to see him. Then, taking a deep breath, I began to unfold my story to him. I told him everything that had happened to me, right up to that very morning, withholding nothing that I thought was of importance. I told him that for various reasons I had kept my illness hidden from everyone in Canada, but now it had got to the point that I felt I was living a lie, and I wanted to share what I had been through. As it all came pouring out, I saw Doris dabbing her eyes as she heard for the first time the full account of the things that I had gone through. She leaned forward, gave me a weak smile and held my hand as I continued.

'The thing is, Pastor,' I gulped as I came to the end of my story, 'I feel so inadequate. I see Christians who I would love to be like, but I feel as though I will never be as strong in the faith as they are.'

Looking at me kindly he got a blank piece of paper out of his desk drawer.

'Draw a line where you feel you are in the Christian life compared to where you see the other people,' he said.

I drew two lines, one some distance away from the other, which represented the Christians I felt I would never be like. He looked at it and then said, 'Now draw a line where you feel you were, say, a year ago.' This time I drew the line even further away from the Christians that I aspired to be like.

'Yes,' he said. 'You're right. You have progressed during the past year, and the progress is what you must concentrate on, not the failings that you are aware of. After all, we all fail from time to time. You have travelled a considerable distance both geographically and spiritually in the last year, Sheila. That's what you need to remind yourself of.'

He was right, of course. But I had other worries. The fact that at one point I had tried to kill myself weighed heavy on my mind, and whatever I tried to do, I couldn't seem to find any relief. I told him the thoughts I was wrestling with, and that I really didn't like myself very much.

Then he said, 'Do you consider yourself bigger than God?'

I looked at him in amazement and said, 'No, of course I don't.'

'Well then,' he said kindly, 'if God loves and has forgiven you, why can't you do the same, and forgive yourself? To do otherwise is in fact putting yourself higher than God. Get in line with what *His* heart and mind is on the subject.'

Again he was right. I was being too hard on myself. He also encouraged me to memorise some scripture verses that I could use in times of trial for encouragement. I felt relieved that I could now put my past behind me, without guilt holding me back from my future.

Now that Doris knew more about my past she was even more of a special friend to me. She did not treat me as an oddity, which was a relief, but as a somebody, doing everything that she could to build me up in the faith. It was good to feel like a someone again, as for a while I had felt more like a ghost, not quite of this world. I shared with Doris how difficult it had been when I wasn't able to read the Bible in the hospital, and look up scriptures that would have given me comfort. The next Sunday she arrived at church with a verse of scripture written in her neat handwriting on a piece of paper. 'Try to memorise this by next week,' she said with a smile. 'That way, if you are ever again in a situation where you don't have access to a Bible, you'll have the scriptures hidden in your heart.' The following Sunday she handed me another scripture, and this went on for the next twelve months, my memory bank of scripture growing each week.

Peter set off in an army coach for Bosnia in April 1994, and with tears in my eyes I waved him goodbye. But I was soon to discover something quite unexpected in Peter's absence. I found that I had a wonderful peace. I missed him greatly – he's my best friend, and I love him dearly – but I did not live in fear each day. I actually experienced an unexpected peace which stayed with me all the time he was away. I'm sure that it was the Lord helping me, but it was also due to the good friends that I now had at church, who rallied round and made sure that I was never alone for long. I knew of course that anyone gets depressed if they mope around, doing nothing, so I made sure that my calendar was full most of the time. Each weekend I would plan an outing with one friend or another. On one occasion I planned a couple of evenings where half of the ladies came round for a chicken and rice meal, with the other half coming round the following week. These were special times when we got to know each other better, and although I missed Peter, I tried to make a negative into a positive.

Doris took advantage of the free local phone calls and rang me every evening just to say 'Hi!' Her house became my second home; Allan must have thought at times that I had moved in! I also had a good friend called Ruby whose husband was away a lot on business. She would ring and find out if I was free to go on a drive with her. We would visit one of the many craft shops that were in that area, followed normally by a visit to a tea shop or ice cream parlour! We shared many a meal and many a laugh! On other occasions I would spend time with another friend, Marion, whose husband was also working away. The invitations came thick and fast. How I appreciated my friends and their thoughtfulness; they brought out the best in me. Hopefully they also gained something from their nutty English friend!

I was eager to grow in my faith as much as I could, so when a retreat was announced I put my name down to go, and then found that the only other person who was able to attend from the church was Doris! We went along anyway, and during that long weekend, I had a growing feeling that the Lord wanted me to share with the church in general the experiences that I had been through, including my mental illness. The opportunity came a little while later, when I was asked to talk at our ladies' meeting. I knew that this was the opportunity that I had been looking for. Although I felt nervous about speaking publicly, I could do it by reading my written words and after much prayer I shared as honestly as I could what I had been through, and how the Lord had helped me.

I didn't know it as I shared with those ladies, but several of them were going through difficult times themselves, and as they came up to speak to me afterwards, giving me a hug or a kiss on the cheek, they told me how much my talk had helped them face their own difficult situations. And none of them thought any the less of me because I had suffered with mental problems, much to my relief.

Peter was now back from Bosnia, and in a few weeks' time we were due to return to Britain. We would both miss Canada, and all the good times and the wonderful friends that we had made. We were returning to Britain having both gone through circumstances which had moulded and changed us to be able to cope with whatever the future held.

21

Trusting God for Tomorrow

We returned to England on an overcast winter's day in December 1994. Peter was about to take up his last posting, having served a total of twenty-five years in the army, eighteen of them married to me. During that time we had lived in nine different houses or flats, not to mention the odd prisoner-of-war camp thrown in for good measure! As we sat in the car outside what was to become home number ten, my mood was as grey as the English weather. It had nothing to do with the house – that was fine. It just happened to be in the wrong location. I wanted it to be in Canada!

People have said to me in the past, 'It must be so easy for you to move, having done it so many times before,' or 'You're lucky to be the sort of person who finds it easy to settle anywhere.' Well, they're wrong! I always find it tough settling into a new place. I had been reluctant to go to Canada, but now we returned with heavy hearts. We had made such good friends over there that saying goodbye for the last time had been particularly painful. But as every army wife knows, one has to overcome negative feelings, and just get on with things. So, just as I had done many times before, I made a definite decision to be positive and turn this house into our home. Feeling sorry for myself for long was not an option I wanted to take up.

Andrew and Laura were still attending boarding school, and it seemed the best thing to let them remain there, especially as we would almost certainly be moving from Dorset when Peter's final posting came to an end. Andrew had GCSEs to take in eighteen months' time and it was essential he had continuity, especially as he found school work hard going, just as I had. 'At least,' I reasoned to myself as I unpacked yet more boxes shortly after the move, 'we are all living in the same country which makes it easier to see each other between terms . . .'

I found this last posting like living in limbo, as I knew it was only a stepping stone into civvy street for us. But we both wanted to put down some spiritual roots as soon as we could, so after visiting various Christian fellowships in the area, we finally joined a small evangelical church, which welcomed us with open arms. The old saying, 'To have a friend means you have to be a friend', is very true. Without effort friendships never mature. They need nurturing, which was always difficult for us in the past, as we seemed to live in each place for such a short space of time. Peter had always settled into a new environment far faster than I did, and our new posting proved to be no exception. Before the week was out he was happily ensconced in his new workplace!

For a little while I found myself lamenting the friendships that were now so far away. But I knew that life had to move on, and I had to advance right along with it. I pulled myself from under my cloud of self-pity, and encouraged myself once again to look on the positive side of life. It was great having my parents living just over an hour away, and we took every opportunity to see them as often as we could. Peter and I began to get really involved with our new church, becoming members, and making lots of new friends.

But what did the future hold? We talked for hours on what life might have in store for us. We weren't sure whether we should move to an area we liked, in the hope of finding work, or just go and live where work became available. Also, Peter was apprehensive about leaving the army. It had after all provided him with employment for nearly all of his working life. A particular Bible verse helped at the time which we found tucked away in Jeremiah 29:11, ' "For I know the plans I have for you," declares the LORD, "plans to prosper you and not to harm you, plans to give you hope and a future." ' We prayed to be open to God's leading, but I have to admit it was not always easy to be patient.

The thought of eventually being able to put down roots, once we had left the army, gave me heady feelings of elation. The army had treated us well enough, but I was growing tired of having to move house every couple of years. I wanted stability, a house where we could all live as a family under the same roof, a dwelling place that was well and truly home for us all. I knew that Peter was hoping that the army would offer him an extension to his army career, but I have to admit that I was praying they would not!

For anyone who hasn't been involved in army life, it's difficult to describe adequately just what a rigmarole one has to go through in something as comparatively straightforward as moving house. Each time we moved, the house we vacated was inspected to check that it was left in pristine condition. An army official would walk around and make sure that all the walls were the same magnolia colour. He would look at every mattress, every carpet, every cupboard, to make sure they were clean and unmarked. The oven had to be taken apart and be spotlessly clean, the bathroom had to shine like the noonday sun! When the children were tiny this was a nightmare, as one or the other would invariably put hand marks on the wall, or spill food in the kitchen, just before an inspection. Weeks before a move we would be packing and cleaning in a frenzy of activity, causing tempers to be fraught and putting relationships under strain. That was one aspect of the army that none of us would miss.

Peter still had a year to go before he was demobbed when one night he came home talking about a job someone had mentioned, in Hereford with the army cadets. 'I've never really been for an interview,' he said, raising his voice slightly so I could hear him as he hung up his coat in the hall, 'so I was thinking of going along, you know, just for the experience. What do you think, love?'

'Do you want this type of job?' I wondered out loud, as I checked the progress of the evening meal. Peter shrugged his shoulders and sat down in his favourite chair by the window. 'I don't know. Probably not,' he said thoughtfully. 'I've still got twelve months to go with the army, so this job won't suit anyway, but maybe I should find out what work *is* suitable for me.'

The next day Peter phoned the number he had been given, and agreed a date for an interview. Next time I was on the phone to Mum and Dad I told them that Peter was keeping his eyes open for future employment, and was following up a job in Hereford, which would be less than two hours away from their house. But the day before the interview, when Peter phoned for directions, he learned that the job was in Hertford in Hertfordshire, not Hereford in Herefordshire. Where on earth was that? A quick look at the map told us that it was just north of London! 'Still, not to worry,' I said as he got ready the next morning, 'it's only an interview, and it's highly unlikely to materialise, is it?'

Well, that's how much I knew! Before we could turn round twice, Peter had been shortlisted, and offered the job, which was due to start six months before he officially left the army. But with holiday leave and the army agreeing to an early release, the job was possible! After a lot of soul-searching, prayer and chewed fingernails, Peter accepted this offer of work. I felt nervous, but also excited at the prospect of a new change of direction in all of our lives. Peter bade a sad farewell to the army, and I tried to sympathise with him, while repressing my desire to leap for joy! I wanted to feel that I belonged somewhere, that our nomadic lifestyle was coming to an end. What elation I felt as we left behind our last army quarter. No more army handovers. Hooray! Peter and I smiled at each other as we drove away from this, our final army house. 'Well, this is the beginning of the rest of our lives,' said Peter, his eyes firmly fixed on the road ahead. 'I wonder what the future holds for us all now?'

We moved into our new house in Hertford as a family. Andrew had by now finished his GCSEs and Laura still had a couple of years before she had to sit her exams. Having two teenagers in the house proved a bit of a challenge, but one we accepted gladly. Living in our own house was something that we all loved, especially as we were able to choose our own colour scheme for the carpets, curtains and walls. And to have a garden that we could make plans for in the years ahead was a real bonus. Our new church is flourishing, and we have begun to plan with others for its future, knowing that we have a part to play in that future. We made many new friends and I am filled with gratitude that we are able to build on those friendships.

Some who read this book may wonder why God allowed us all to go through the situations that I have written about,

211

especially as we have put our faith and trust in Him. But the fact is that everyone will probably experience trials and tribulations in one form or another in their lives, maybe through the agony of bereavement, the pain of broken relationships, the threat of insecurity or illness. These are all common human sufferings. And just like every other member of the human race, I am not immune to any of them. Being a Christian doesn't stop us going through troubles, but it does mean that we go through the circumstances with Him. He said, 'I will never leave you or forsake you.' Like a good shepherd He will guide His lost sheep right into the fold of life eternal, if only we trust Him, and ask Him for forgiveness and help.

My own testing times were no joy-ride, but strangely enough they have ultimately blessed my life and strengthened my faith. What we go through is probably not as important as how we react to what we go through. Do our adverse experiences cause us to be a better person – or a bitter person? I'll be honest and say that I would not have chosen the route my life took. My choice would have been sunshine and roses all the way! But it's often in the midst of trouble, when we are at our weakest point, that we find out the most about ourselves. What I discovered was that I can't do everything on my own – I'm not strong enough – but that I don't have to! I learnt how to let go of my self-sufficiency and replace it with God-dependency. I count myself as fortunate. God has been good to me.

I have met many people as we have travelled from pillar to post, sadly far too many to mention in this book. Each person has touched my life in some way, some of course more than others. If you're one of the many people who have played a part in my story that I have not been able to mention, due to lack of space, I want you to know that you are not forgotten, but remembered with fondness in the recesses of my heart and mind.

I know that God is still working in my life, and making me into the kind of person that He wants me to be. I am aware that sometimes I allow my lack of confidence and my shyness to hold me back from stepping out of my comfort zone, but even with all my imperfections I know that I am loved by God. I am accepted for the person that I am, not the person that I would aspire to be. That's the kind of powerful love that God offers to me, no matter what happens in the future. In the New Testament, the question is asked, 'Who shall separate us from the love of Christ? Shall trouble or hardship or persecution or famine or nakedness or danger or sword?' Then the powerful statement is made in reply, **'For I am convinced that neither death nor life, neither angels nor demons, neither the present nor the future, nor any powers, neither height nor depth, nor anything else in all creation, will be able to separate us from the love of God that is in Christ Jesus our Lord'** (Romans 8:35, 38).

I love these verses. During those times when fears and uncertainties come calling, as I read them they remind me that God has His hand upon my life. Even when God seems so far away, it's only because my problems are blocking Him from view. Like the clouds which so often hide the sun, it doesn't mean that the sun has 'gone walkabout' because it's out of sight, it's where it has always been, shining high in the sky. In the same way, just because I may not feel God's presence, it doesn't alter the fact that He is still with me, even if my confused feelings may be telling me differently. The Christian faith does not depend upon feelings but upon facts.

For me the pathway of life is an exciting journey, to be taken one step at a time. Maybe I will have a recurrence of my post-traumatic stress disorder at some time in the future, or some other unseen drama may raise its ugly head. But I refuse to live my life in fear of a lot of possible 'what ifs'. I don't know what the future holds, but I now know the One who does, which gives me confidence and hope for tomorrow. May you also find hope, that will carry you through the storms of your life and through your worst nightmares, bringing you safely to the other side.